SUSAN CROSBY
THE MATING GAME

Wishing you
a lifetime o
romance

Susan Crosby
1994

SILHOUETTE *Desire*

Published by Silhouette Books
America's Publisher of Contemporary Romance

To the men in my life:
David and Kevin, who make motherhood a joy
beyond compare.
Jerry, Steve and Tom, brothers extraordinaire,
who tease, support and cheer.
And mostly to Ken, my own hero, the most enthusiastic
research assistant in the world. Thanks for the patience,
the faith, the friendship and the love.
I'd marry you all over again.

 SILHOUETTE BOOKS

ISBN 0-373-05888-8

THE MATING GAME

Copyright © 1994 by Susan Bova Crosby

Printed in U.S.A.

SUSAN CROSBY

loves to set goals for herself. "Publish a romance" has been on her to-do list the longest, and she's delighted to cross it off and let the next long-term goal head up the list: "Publish another romance." She loves holing up in her office to create warm, strong heroes and good-hearted, self-reliant heroines.

She and her husband of twenty-seven years have two grown sons and live in the Central Valley of California, close enough to San Francisco to occasionally appreciate the hustle and bustle of big-city life but savoring day-to-day life in a smaller town. She spent a mere seven and a half years getting through college and finally crossed "Earn BA in English" off her to-do list a few years ago. She's worked as a synchronized swimming instructor, a personnel interviewer at a toy factory and a trucking company manager. Variety, she says, makes for more interesting novels!

Susan loves to hear from readers. You can write to her care of Silhouette Books, 300 E. 42nd Street, New York, NY 10017.

Dear Reader,

Mazatlán, Mexico, holds wonderful memories for me. I was nine years old on my first visit, when the tiny oceanside city offered a choice of only two motels. Recently, my husband and I celebrated our twenty-fifth anniversary there, a town now teeming with hotels but still boasting warm Pacific waters and genial people.

What a great place to set a romance, I thought, envisioning an intense, cautious man meeting an outgoing, trusting woman while vacationing in paradise. Thus, *The Mating Game* was born. But fictional characters don't get *all* the luck. I've been living a fairy tale since a telephone call changed my life: "We'd like to buy your book," said editor Melissa Jeglinski. Stunned, I eventually mumbled "Wow," or some similarly intelligent response. My feet had almost touched ground again when three weeks later Melissa said, "Congratulations! You're our 1994 Premiere author for Desire." *Wow!*

A longtime reader of romance novels, I have definite opinions on the genre. I appreciate how romances celebrate men and women, as individuals and as couples—how the hero loses none of his strength when the woman he loves sees him vulnerable, and how the heroine loses none of her softness when the man she loves sees her negotiate a tough business deal. Primary in their relationship is respect, as in any enduring relationship.

I read romances to celebrate life and to mentally vacation somewhere new. I hope *The Mating Game* lets you do the same.

Susan Crosby

expectation of parole. Julia told Wes that Kani needed a dose of happiness, too, her life having also become empty.

It took three weeks to make the arrangements, but when Julia hung up the phone late one Wednesday evening in June, a smile of satisfaction curved lazily on her lips.

"All set?" her husband asked.

"Their hooks have been baited."

Wes grinned and stretched languidly beside his wife, their son nestled between them and nursing greedily at her breast. "I hope they have half as much fun getting acquainted as we did. But if nothing else, at least they will have had a brief vacation away from their troubles."

Twelve long days would pass before they would know the results. . . .

Prologue

With amazing frequency, the moment newlyweds emerge from their cocoon of honeymoon ecstasy, they begin casting their eyes toward an unsuspecting potential twosome and a goal of comparable happiness. And if life were fair, warnings would be issued to all unmarried persons of consenting age, advising them to run for cover if acquainted with a couple newly married and gloriously happy.

Life is not always fair.

Wes and Julia Linnell had been married a year and a half when they were struck severely by The Curse of Marital Bliss.

Call it fate, call it serendipity—call it incredible bad luck for the two unsuspecting and unacquainted old friends who happened to contact Julia and Wes on the very same day—for the blissful Linnell couple began to plot a happy resolution for the previously content-to-be-single Kani Warner and Iain MacKenzie.

Wes told Julia that Iain's life had become so barren he was living in a dark cell of hopelessness with no immediate

One

———

Iain MacKenzie had no idea why he'd been gifted with an all-expense-paid trip to Mazatlán, Mexico, but he figured he was due a little pleasure. How many losses was one man supposed to take, anyway?

Maybe his accountant had been the anonymous benefactor. Yeah, right. Sure. *And I'm William Shakespeare.*

It had been a hell of a month. First he'd been fired, then, in the same week, he'd found out his longtime friend and trusted accountant had embezzled all but a few thousand dollars from his checking account. Iain had lived frugally for twelve years, saving the majority of his earnings. All that money—gone.

Thirty-two years old and what the hell did he have to show for his time and effort? An aborted career, a condo that had only depreciated in value in a soft Los Angeles real estate market, and no glowing letter of recommendation.

The adversarial relationship between Iain and fellow writer Darcy Johansen on the daytime serial "A Time to Love" had escalated into full war when Darcy was promoted to head writer. The first item on her agenda had been to fire Iain over "creative differences," leaving a writing staff composed entirely of women.

What really galled him was that he'd finally earned enough clout and credibility as a writer on the daytime serial to introduce some serious topics. Of course he'd paid his dues to reach that point. It had been his brilliant idea, after all, to have an alien impregnate the ingenue, Sapphire Sheridan, thus offering daytime TV its first virgin birth. Or so it had seemed until Lance Beauregard had gone public with his hypnosis skills and proudly displayed a birthmark that matched the alien baby's Saturn-shaped pattern on his left buttock.

Yeah, Iain had been proud of that story line, really proud. He snorted aloud, drawing a curious glance from the young man seated beside him on the airplane. *Careful, old man,* he cautioned himself. *Your cynicism is reaching new depths, even for you.*

As the plane shuddered to a stop near the Mazatlán airport terminal, he dug out a white envelope from his carry-on bag and examined it for probably the tenth time. No clues whatsoever. Whoever had sent him the plane ticket and voucher covering room and board never intended that he discover the identity of his fairy godmother. Specific instructions on traveling from the airport to the hotel were typed on blank stationery, along with a personal postscript: "No strings. Just enjoy yourself at our expense. Have fun!"

Have fun. A simple two-word directive. Simple for most people, he supposed. But life wasn't so simple for him. Never had been. Never would be.

The passengers spilled out of the plane to a blast of hot air. Heat and poverty. It was a smell Iain realized he'd never forget. He lifted his face to the scorching midday sun. What the hell. He might as well enjoy this vacation.

What else did he have to lose?

* * *

Kani Warner stood staring at her open suitcase. Trance-like, she retrieved her baggage check from her airline ticket envelope and matched the numbers to the tag dangling from the handle of the suitcase on the hotel room bed. They matched. How could that be?

Nothing looked familiar. Nothing. Where were the denim shorts and cotton blouse she had packed on top? Where was the five-year-old pink-and-orange maillot swimsuit she'd rolled like a sausage to cushion her hair dryer?

Gingerly she lifted a blue envelope from atop a frothy bit of white satin and lace. A handwritten note solved the dilemma: "Kani—I took the liberty of providing you with a few new vacation clothes. Thank goodness you're so easy to fit! Don't worry about Gypsy. We'll take good care of her. You take good care of yourself. Julia."

Well, at least Kani knew now why Julia had been acting so strangely this morning. Kani's Uncle Henry had given her this trip to Mazatlán, and when she'd called her good friend Julia to tell her the news, Julia had volunteered to keep her kitten, Gypsy, while she was away. Julia had even insisted Kani spend the night to accustom Gypsy to the new residence with Kani there, then she had taken Kani to the San Francisco airport this morning.

Thinking back, Kani could pinpoint the moment Julia had switched the contents of her suitcase. She had plopped her infant son in Kani's arms and retreated to the nursery, leaving Kani to jiggle, rock and sing to the adorable raven-haired boy until Julia came down the stairs, Kani's suitcase in one hand, a diaper bag in the other. Yes, Julia had been upstairs long enough to empty the well-worn clothing out of the luggage and replace it with . . . what?

Investigating the contents, Kani discovered everything she'd tried on and liked, but couldn't afford to buy, during a recent shopping expedition with Julia. Three—three!—bathing suits: a sleek maillot and two bikinis, each with bra-style cups and French-cut legs. Four pairs of shorts, six blouses, two skirts, three sundresses—when would she wear all of this? Then there were bras and camisoles and bikini underwear, all matching, all soft and sexy.

There were at least six nightgowns in varying styles, some revealing, some not. And, goodness, two—not one, but two—boxes of condoms!

Kani started to laugh, a box in each hand. Oh, Julia, you delightful, hopeful friend, you! As if she'd ever sleep with a stranger met on vacation. Not Kani Warner. Definitely not.

She'd had it with men, anyway. A woman just couldn't count on them. They teased and enticed and said all the right things, playing their male games. Then, as soon as either the *L* word or the *C* word was uttered, they became masters of the quick getaway. Love and commitment meant nothing.

Kani could confirm the theory, all right. Men do give love to get sex. And she supposed women do give sex to get love. Do we really play so many games with each other? she wondered. Is anyone honest?

Yes, of course. There were plenty of honest people in the world. She just hadn't met a male one yet.

Methodically she put the clothes away, admiring each item like an orphan savoring unhoped-for Christmas gifts. Lifting a soft silk nightie from the dresser drawer, Kani wandered into the living room of her suite and slid open the sliding glass doors. A strong, steady breeze, salty and damp, blew against her face. She stepped onto the fourth-floor balcony to take in the spectacular view of the ocean. Unconsciously she rubbed the silk against her face and down her throat, reveling in the sensuous glide of fabric.

Leaning her elbows against the railing, she watched as children played in the sand, teenagers surfed on boogie boards and adults became kids again. The joyful sounds drifted to her balcony, wrapped her in a cocoon of enchantment and tugged at her to join the other pleasure seekers in the warm Pacific waters. Her clothes were stripped off before she'd reached the bedroom, and she slipped into the neon green maillot, shaking her head at the unsubtle color.

She closed her suitcase and tucked it away in the closet, tucking away her troubles, too. *I'm not going to think about it,* she decided. The most important thing in her life, her dearly beloved Ramshackle Theater, was soon to be just another statistic, a brief and shining moment, just like Camelot. She'd poured her heart and soul into the tiny theater—and all of her money, besides. Her efforts to subsidize the losing proposition had come to an end. Her only concern now was that she close the theater with a special production, something memorable for herself and all those people who had been involved for the last seven years.

But not this week. No, not this week. This week she would have fun, and relax, and forget her problems. Into the closet they went, along with the suitcase, not to be opened again until the end of the week. Surely she'd earned that much!

Iain sat on the low wall separating the beach from the hotel patio. After twenty minutes of resting there, he dubbed the concrete barricade The Wall of Imminent Resistance, a barrier meant to keep at bay the constant stream of vendors flowing across the hot sand. Obviously the vendors weren't allowed to appeal to the hotel guests beyond vocal range; instead, they offered ingenious sales pitches as they leaned against the wall and held up jewelry cases, hats, T-shirts, carved wooden animals and other can't-live-without-'em tourist enticements.

"Come on down! Let's make a deal," a grinning vendor called, drawing laughs from the large group of vacationers relaxing under *palapas,* grass shade umbrellas. He set his black jewelry-filled briefcase on the wall. Silver earrings sparkled like lures to unwary fish; bracelets gleamed with the shimmering aura of a rising sun. Two women, their skin prevacation pale, moved from the shade to the wall, ready to negotiate.

Iain glanced around, noting many untanned bodies. Had everyone arrived today? Monday seemed an odd day for everyone to be just getting there.

Wait a minute! His gaze swept the entire patio, which circled a small pool and stretched past an open dining area and beyond, where three long rows of lounge chairs marked the end of the hotel property.

Iain slapped a hand to his forehead. Great, this was just great. He'd been given an all-expense-paid trip to a time-share condominium resort, the kind frequented by baby-boomer couples vacationing with their sombrero-shaded parents and their designer-clothed children. His perusal of the patio led to an obvious conclusion: every female here was either too young, too old, or too married.

Gee, thanks, Fairy Godmother. Thanks for a week alone.

Not that being alone was anything new for Iain. But, hell, alone he would just focus on his problems. That wasn't the point of this vacation, was it? He could have been depressed at home.

"¿Señor?"

Iain's head spun toward the polite voice. A young man extended a tray.

The beer he'd ordered. Great. This he needed. Desperately. He penned in a tip before signing the tab, then his hand encircled the cool bottle and tilted it to his mouth. Ahhh. Wonderful.

He was lowering the bottle and opening his eyes when he spotted a woman in a brilliant green swimsuit strolling from the shore toward the hotel patio.

Sleek. It was the only word to describe her. Wet, dark hair trailed down her back in one long braid. Smooth Lycra fabric molded a body of slender curves and valleys—breasts that would more than fill a man's palms, a waist his hands could almost span, hips that flared enticingly. The French-cut suit emphasized trim thighs that stretched almost endlessly. Skin the color of rich café au lait and dotted with salt water shimmered in the sun's rays. She crouched to inspect a sand castle two little girls were building, and he watched her muscles respond and tighten. She wasn't brawny, but every muscle had definition. Sexy. Very, very sexy.

She scooped up some wet sand and drizzled it over the lopsided mound the children had created, and they laughed at something she said. Hefting a pink plastic bucket, she sauntered to a knee-high depth and dipped the pail into the gentle waves. Lord, what an incredibly sexy walk she had! Slinky and slow, her taut buttocks all silken sinew.

Returning to the castle, she set the bucket on the sand, then began digging a hole next to the mound. Her swimsuit drooped away from her body, revealing paler skin where her tan ended, skin that heralded the firm flesh of perfect breasts. And when she sat up straight and shaded her eyes with her hand to watch a parasailer drift to a landing near her on the beach, the slender form in the magnetic neon swimsuit raised Iain's temperature several degrees.

He sucked in a deep breath, attempting to shatter his focus. Undoubtedly she was here with someone. In fact, the two little girls might be hers. Mesmerized, he couldn't stop his gaze from following her as she waved to the girls, climbed the stairs to the patio, and paused to wash the sand off her feet under a faucet.

Then somehow she was standing right in front of him, and his eyes again focused on the brilliantly colored fabric before tracing a slow, hot path upward.

"Is it good? Do you like it?" she asked.

For a wordsmith, he became incredibly inept at the English language. "Huh?"

She laughed. "The beer. That's the local brand, right? I was curious if it's any good."

Iain turned the bottle in his hand and lifted it toward his face. Pacifico. Oh, yeah, the locally made brew. Was it good? Hell, he'd drunk the whole thing and never even tasted it.

He glanced back up at her—American accent, hair the color of mink shot with gold, cocoa brown eyes sprinkled with gold dust and tilted enticingly, cover girl cheekbones, soft lips and very white teeth . . . that were sparkling in an amused smile at him.

"I didn't realize the questions were so tough," she commented.

Iain wiped a hand down his face, attempting to remove the love-smitten schoolboy expression he knew had to be on it. "Guess I needed this vacation more than I thought. The beer's fine." *I hope.*

"Thanks. I'll give it a try."

She turned to go. Iain stopped her with a hand on her arm. Her muscles bunched then relaxed. "May I buy you a beer?"

"No. But thanks for asking."

Then she was gone—to her boyfriend or husband or whatever, he supposed. Resisting the urge to sulk, he deliberately turned away from her retreating form. Spotting a volleyball game farther down the beach, he unfolded his legs off the wall and moved toward the players, wanting to vent his frustration in competition and challenge. There were plenty of other women around at the other hotels, he decided. He'd check out the scene tonight.

He stopped himself from turning back to seek out the bewitching water sprite again. There were plenty of other mermaids in the sea.

Thank you, Uncle Henry, Kani thought as she stood under the shower's warm flow, her skin tingling from the afternoon of sun and salt water. She felt utterly relaxed. And something else . . .

Sensitized. Every cell, every follicle, every neuron had come to attention this afternoon, as if letting go of the problems at home had allowed her senses to declare a mutiny. She ran soap-slicked palms down her torso and closed her eyes, savoring the pinpricks of sensitivity. She couldn't ever remember feeling this way before—so *hungry* for touch.

She didn't know why she was experiencing this sudden craving. She'd gone years at a stretch without sex since her first uncomfortable experience in Jimmy Moore's sedan her senior year in high school. Since then she'd had two fairly long-term relationships, thought she'd been in love with both of them, then had been— unceremoniously—dumped.

The sex had been okay, although not spectacular. It had been nice, warm and comfortable, if a little disappointing. She had given it her best effort, invested a lot of herself in the relationships both in and out of bed, but it hadn't made a difference in the long run. She didn't have that special something it took to hold on to a man.

Snap out of it, Kani. No feeling sorry for yourself this week.

Kani shut off the warm water and rinsed her hair in pure cold, adding extra shine to her already gleaming locks. Should she braid it? Put it in a ponytail? Leave it down? It was hot and humid outside the air-conditioned room; she was afraid she'd sweat too much with her cloak of thick curls covering her back. And yet . . . and yet she felt sexiest with it down.

Now why would that matter to you, Kani Warner? You're not here for sex. You're here for . . . what?

Peace, relaxation, freedom, change of pace were supposed to be her goals. But being here with a special man would make it perfect!

It was fun choosing an outfit to wear to dinner, from lingerie outward. She'd bought few new clothes in the past several years and certainly nothing as frivolous as the white lace push-up bra and matching underwear, or the dress of ivory cotton that whispered over her skin, swirled around her calves and dipped low over her breasts.

It really was a shame there was no one to show off her new wardrobe for, she thought with a rueful smile. Good old Uncle Henry. This was his idea of a perfect vacation, she supposed. But had he forgotten she was single and might like to flirt with some unattached men of her own age? Even socializing with other single women would be fun and would give her someone to explore the city with. Four years of high school Spanish gave her a working knowledge of the language, but she wasn't foolish enough to go wandering about on her own.

It might be kind of fun to explore that very attractive, if somewhat dense, man she'd spoken to this afternoon. He'd been close to six foot, she supposed, although it was hard to tell since he'd been seated. His sun-streaked chestnut hair had been combed straight back, the length curling down the nape of his neck, an invitation to feminine fingers to muss and comb. Dark sunglasses had hidden his eyes, but his mouth—goodness, his mouth—had looked...soft and enticing, his jaw well-defined, his smooth-shaven chin punctuated with a shallow cleft. He was lean and fit. There was good muscle tone in his long legs, his shoulders were very broad and his chest enticing—firmly muscled and lightly dusted with sun-bleached hair.

Too bad he could hardly seem to string a complete sentence together.

He'd asked if he could buy her a beer. Did that mean he was single, or yet another attached male looking for a temporary conquest? Although it was hard to imagine a single man at this family resort, it wasn't impossible. After all, she was here, right?

At least her chances of meeting someone involved in show business were minimal. That was a mistake she would never repeat.

Two

The flyer she'd been given at the front desk announced a welcome party at poolside before dinner. Kani glided into the group of guests juggling drinks and bowls of popcorn, accepted a margarita, declined the popcorn, then sat on a lounge chair near the concrete wall dividing the patio from the beach.

The sun would be setting soon, and she hoped it would be spectacular. She wanted to toast the brilliant colors, and Uncle Henry, and her dear friend Julia...and maybe have a couple more drinks and toast her erstwhile lovers, love and commitment—and bury them once and for all. Then perhaps she'd plant herself at a table on the open patio and splurge on an extravagant dinner while holding herself aloof, being mysterious in her aloneness. People would whisper about the woman in white who looked untouchable and sad.

The image made her laugh. She loved people and would not be convincing as a lady of mystery. For all her acting experience, she never seemed to be able to maintain a role offstage. It would be more like her to barge in on a table full of people and ask if she could sit with them.

"¿Señorita?" a small voice queried.

Kani focused on the boy standing before her. He was seven or eight, she decided, and had the sweetest face she'd ever seen, with a smile so soft it melted her heart. He held out a red rose just on the verge of opening. "For you, *señorita.*"

"Muchas gracias. How lovely." She pressed it to her nose and inhaled deeply.

"De el señor," the boy said.

Kani followed the boy's pointing finger. "From what man?"

"Allí. There."

Ah! The dense but gorgeous beach god raised his glass in a small toast to her. She smiled and lifted the rose, nodding her thanks.

His hands were surprisingly elegant as he wordlessly invited her to join him at his table. She had already started to stand when the boy suddenly whipped around her and leapt over the wall. She watched him run laughing up the beach as the security guard shouted at him in words Kani couldn't follow.

"He wasn't bothering me," she said to the guard.

"Is not allowed, *señorita.*"

"He's just a child."

"Sí, señorita. There are many children. There are rules. For the comfort of our guests, *señorita.*"

Kani's mouth tightened.

"Problem?" The sender of the rose materialized beside her. "Are you all right?"

"Yes, thank you. The guard chased the boy off."

"It's a game they play, I think. The boy had his eye on the guard every second he was over the wall. And I honestly think the guard knew he was there and chose his moment to chase him."

"You do? You mean they like playing cat and mouse?"

"I think so, yes." Iain's hands itched to touch her incredible hair, so long and thick and curling. "Are you actually here alone?"

Kani turned to him, closing the curtains on the little drama between the boy and the guard. Turquoise. His eyes were turquoise. Deep, bright, clear. Long, dark lashes. Sleepy lids. Sexy lids. This could mean trouble. Especially now that she knew he was more than an extra from an old Gidget movie.

She sighed deeply. With great reluctance and a sense of inevitability she extended her hand. "Hi. I'm Kani Warner. And yes, I'm here alone."

He accepted her proffered hand, then closed his other hand over their grip. "Iain MacKenzie. I'm here alone, too." *Thank God!*

"What were you toasting as the sun set awhile back?" Iain asked when they were settled at his table and had ordered fresh drinks.

"The incredible colors."

He cocked his head at her, scrutinizing her expression. "What else?"

Kani shifted in her chair. "I was also toasting my uncle, who gave me this trip, and a good friend who made it even more special."

"What else?"

Her fingertips traveled lightly across the edge of the table, memorizing the bumpy feel of the painted wrought iron. "That's all."

"Your expression was more wistful than that."

Uh-oh. Really big trouble—a perceptive as well as an attractive man. "Losses," she replied finally.

Iain hid his surprise, unwilling to reveal they had something in common. In his experience, once a woman knew he was suffering from any emotional upheaval, she began acting like a police detective with a suspect in custody. The white light would focus on his face as questions were fired at him with machine-gun speed, demanding he spill his guts. In his experience, it was a biological impossibility for a woman to let a man work out his own problems; they always insisted that he share his problems, that he'd feel better getting it off his chest. It's okay to be sensitive, they would say.

Right. Be sensitive, but don't dare stop being strong, either. But he'd learned his lesson the hard way—don't share because they never let you forget it.

Kani's smile was deceptively sweet. "And no, I don't want to talk about it. I promised myself a week away from problems."

"Fine. I won't push you, and you won't push me, okay?"

"Were you toasting losses, too?"

"I hadn't lifted my glass yet."

The waiter set their drinks in front of them—two margaritas, one rimmed with salt, one not.

Kani raised her glass. "To better times."

"To the week ahead." Iain touched his glass to hers, transferring a sample of his salt onto the edge of her heavy goblet. Before she could sip, he grasped the stem and slowly spun her glass until the white crystals hovered before her lips. With his fingertip he tilted the drink toward her. Their gazes locked as she sipped and swallowed, then her tongue made a slow sweep of her lips, catching the salt.

He mimicked her, savoring his own salt slowly, teasingly. Only the sound of the surf pounded in their ears. Together they tasted salt . . . and desire. Together they acknowledged each other's pull, magnetic and energizing.

Together—the word held all sorts of possibilities.

Kani set her goblet down with a quiet *thump,* disconcerted and more than a little aroused. She'd flirted a lot in her life and acknowledged it as a basic personality trait, an attribute that made her good at her day job as a bartender, earning her extra tips and repeat customers. But she couldn't remember feeling this urgent draw toward a man, ever.

She also knew when to make a safe retreat and let the situation defuse itself. "Is this your first visit to Mazatlán, Iain?"

Iain smiled, playing along with her but letting her know she wasn't fooling him. "First time."

"What made you come here?"

"My fairy godmother arranged it. I just followed instructions."

"Your fairy godmother?"

"Someone—I don't know who—decided I needed a vacation. I didn't ask questions."

"I guess that eliminates mob connections," Kani said, before leaning back in her chair to more easily observe his lanky frame.

"How do you figure that?"

"If you'd been worried about being bumped off, you'd have gone off in another direction."

He smiled. "A rather dramatic concept. Are you a writer?"

"Bartender."

Now *that* interested him. He leaned forward, resting his forearms against the table. "Really. Where?"

"In San Francisco. At one of the big hotels."

"Do you like it?"

"Absolutely. I love it. Great job. Great city. How about you?"

He took a long drink first. "I live in Los Angeles. I'm sort of between jobs."

Kani's shoulders dropped. Well, that was that. Another one down the drain. She had really had it with these men who couldn't keep jobs. Iain had to be thirty years old. He should have a career, be stable, be ready for children, for heaven's sake. Unless he already—

"Are you married?" she blurted out. "Do you have children?"

He had watched her digest the information that he was unemployed, her expression revealing a flash of disgust. Hell, *he* was disgusted. But God, he was sick and tired of women standing in judgment of him or interfering in his life.

He'd be damned if he'd let this slip of a woman look down her straight little nose at him. He shattered his own

rule against sharing anything personal—because for some
bewildering reason her opinion meant more to him than he
wanted to admit.

He leaned threateningly toward her until she shrank back.
"You couldn't pay me to shackle myself to any woman. I
wouldn't dream of bringing a child into this screwed-up
world. And I'm unemployed because of the whims of a
woman who felt threatened by my competence. I don't live
in Los Angeles. I live in Hollywood, so that ought to lower
me further in your estimation. But you know something,
lady? I don't care. I don't give a damn what you think."

He tossed his napkin onto the table as he stood. "Have a
nice evening."

Kani was so stunned by the verbal barrage she almost
didn't react in time. As it was, she caught only the hem of
his shorts, her hand brushing the crisp hair on his thigh.

"Iain," she said quietly, "I'm sorry. I'm the last person
to stand in judgment of anyone. Please." She knew he was
also upset at having revealed so much of himself to her.

Feeling ridiculously like a petulant child in the midst of a
grocery-store tantrum, Iain forced himself to sit carefully in
the chair he'd just vacated.

Kani slid her hand under the table to grasp his and en-
countered bare skin—electrifying, tantalizing skin. She
fumbled a bit to find his hand. "You're not making this easy
on me," she said, chiding.

A reluctant smile was wrenched from him. "I could tell
you you're making it damned hard on me, but I wouldn't be
so crude." He caught her wandering hand in his and
squeezed. "I overreacted. I apologize. It's been a hell of a
month."

"Betcha mine's been worse."

"Has not."

"Has, too."

They grinned at each other, then Iain lifted her hand,
turning it to press his lips to the pulsing blue vein crossing
her delicate wrist.

He couldn't have known how vulnerable she was—how long it had been since anyone had been gentle with her, how long since she'd been quietly seduced or treated like porcelain. How long she had hungered for someone to care for her, love her, cherish her. *Are you the one, Iain? Are you? What am I going to do with these feelings if you're not?*

As soon as he lifted his head, she placed her free hand over the spot he'd kissed, trapping the warmth. "I have a confession to make," she said. "When I spoke with you this afternoon, I decided you were gorgeous but mindless. I'm so glad I was wrong. Well, you're still gorgeous—"

"You dazzled me," he said quietly. "You dazzled me speechless."

Oh, breath, come back! She gulped for air. "But I'm so average."

Iain laughed. "Average. You." He didn't say the words as questions but as statements of disbelief.

"Always," she confirmed with a nod. "Average height, average weight, plain brown hair and eyes. Average."

Iain cataloged her as she spoke and rewrote the description: just tall enough to tuck her head under his chin; a body so far beyond average it could set new standards for it; hair so lustrous and tempting he craved to bury his hands in it, wanted to let it fall around them like a curtain as they made love; and eyes that fairly shimmered with radiance and joy and zest. She enjoyed life; everything she said or did, every expression on her face broadcast it. She probably couldn't walk past a hopscotch chalked on a sidewalk. *Will you help me rise to your level, Kani? God, please don't let me make her sink to mine.*

The waiter made a timely arrival, bringing their dinners and dispelling the tension. They settled into eating before speaking again. Kani liked the comfortable silence; it boded well that neither felt they had to speak all the time.

Iain stabbed the last shrimp on his plate and shook it at her as he broke the stretch of silence. "You know, you don't look like a Constance."

"I'm not. My name is spelled *K-a-n-i*. It's Hawaiian, after my grandmother."

"Ah, mystery solved." He wiggled a finger at her face. "The tilt to your oh-so-average eyes."

She couldn't help but laugh at his obvious sarcasm. "My grandfather met my grandmother in Honolulu during World War II. They had two children, my mother and my uncle, Henry."

"The one who gave you this trip."

"Right. My father died fourteen years ago. My mother remarried and lives in Tucson, Arizona."

"You get along with your mother?"

"Oh, yes. With my stepfather, too. He's a gem. She's somewhat of a scatterbrain, but he just follows behind her, fixing what she knocks over, putting away what she leaves out, providing her with lists of errands to do. She's childlike in many ways, but dear and sweet. My brother and I feel fortunate to have her, to have both of them. Tell me more about you."

Iain shoved his plate away. "My name's spelled a little differently, too. *I-a-i-n*. It's Gaelic, a pretension of my mother's, who sought bigger and better things all her life."

"Past tense? She isn't alive?"

"I've seen her only once in the past twenty-six years. I don't expect to see her again." *For fifteen years, I thought she was dead. Even my father let me think so. She is dead to me. Dead and buried.*

"I'm sorry. And your father?"

"He works as a cameraman for a number of game shows. We don't see a lot of each other. No siblings."

Sounds lonely. Kani caught herself before uttering the words aloud. He had spoken matter-of-factly about his life, but she caught an undertone of anger and sadness and maybe even longing. *Do you need a family, Iain? Someone to care for? Someone to make up for what was missing in your own life?*

She watched him drum his fingers on the table, obviously uneasy with the conversation. She took pity on him. "Did you take a taxi from the airport?"

Iain laughed and nodded, grateful for the change of subject. "I take it that you did, too? Wasn't that an adventure? Man, I thought for sure the bottom of the cab would fall off before we got here."

"No such thing as shock absorbers, I guess. I swear I could feel the road under my feet. Did your driver break any rules?"

"Are there any here? By California standards, he did. Too many to count. I felt like an airplane passenger who'd gotten off a harrowing flight. I wanted to kiss the ground."

"I know, I know. Thank goodness I rode in with a couple who come here frequently. It would have scared me to death, but they had prepared me for it. I just had to fight laughing out loud."

Kani shifted a little to allow the waiter to pick up her empty plate as she refused dessert. She reached for the tab at the same time as Iain. "We can split it."

He glanced at her after he'd signed the check. "You can buy breakfast."

Kani smiled slowly, pleased that she could count on tomorrow.

"Would you like to take a walk on the beach?" he asked as they stood. "I asked around earlier. People say it's safe."

She couldn't say why she trusted him, only that she did. Maybe it was the pain he tried so hard to hide; maybe it was that moment of vulnerability he'd shown her. Maybe it was a lot more complicated than that.

Whatever the reason, she believed in him. She let her hand slip into his and closed her eyes briefly to savor the flash of longing that traveled up her arm and channeled down her torso directly to her womb, and beyond. *Pheromones. It's just pheromones.* Those lovely little uncontrollable, undefinable scents and chemical attractants. Goodness, this man feels wonderful!

But it was moving all too fast.

"I'm really tired, Iain. The traveling and the sun..."

"One dance before you turn in?"

The music came from a solo performer, a keyboardist who also sang tunes ranging from "La Bamba" to "My Way"—not exactly the hit parade, but atmospheric.

She should have known he'd be a superb dancer, the best dancer she'd ever partnered. He led easily; she followed gracefully. Their thighs brushed, retreated, brushed again, each time notching their temperatures up a fraction. The fingers of his right hand were splayed against the small of her back, keeping her close and gently telegraphing the next move. Her right hand lay solidly in his left and he tightened his grip as he spun them around in a dazzling move.

Kani banished conscious thought to the palm trees and gave herself to physical sensation. This man can dance! She felt seduced as his knee bent and glided between hers, drawing her more snugly to him, his fingertips skimming farther around her to graze her ribs. He flattened her right hand against his chest and encircled her with both arms, his palms at her waist measuring the enticing indentation, then sliding with exquisite slowness to press into the upper curve of her buttocks, pulling her against him.

Every maneuver was handled with such finesse, such grace, such flair, that they never misstepped, never broke the rhythm of the music, never let the soaring sensations slip. The warm, humid air sizzled with their heat until their skin was dewy and their sultry scents rose to entice, tease, torment... *promise*.

Iain kept her within his arms but lifted his hands to grab fistfuls of her hair and rub the soft curls until he'd created static electricity. The fragrance of lemons wafted from her hair to mingle with her own particular scent, and Iain dropped his head back, fighting the need to kiss her.

One week. They had only one week. Part of him wanted to spend it all in bed with her. Part of him wanted to make memories, wanted to seduce slowly, create a scene she wouldn't forget, that *he* wouldn't forget.

"I love the way you smell," she said.

Iain groaned at the quivering words breathed against his chest as her nose pressed the moist skin where throat met collarbone. He angled his head down until his mouth touched her ear. "I would suggest you get the hell out of here before I—" The words that followed were more than suggestive, but direct and flattering.

And oh-so-tempting, Kani thought, tipping her head to see for herself the rigid control she felt in his words and his body.

Iain briefly analyzed the aroused curiosity on her face, then his gaze dipped to covet her breasts, pushed high and round. He inhaled deeply, reveling in her steamy fragrance, which beckoned like fire pulling in air to breathe and flare. Her tongue darted out to moisten her lips and her mouth moved, but no sound came.

Good night. The words jammed in her mind. She tried again. *Good night, Iain.* She gave up, settled for a brush of her hand down his cheek and the touch of her thumb to his lips.

Then, like dandelion seeds in the wind, she swept out of his arms and away.

She was out of breath, panting as if she'd done an hour of aerobics, while she fitted the key to the suite. Struggling to unlock the door to her room, she fumbled, stopped and closed her eyes. Taking a deep breath, she carefully guided the key into the lock and turned the knob. She walked directly to the balcony, flung open the doors and launched herself against the railing.

Oh my. There had been people all around them—guests and employees, even the damned singer! They'd practically made love on the dance floor. She pushed her hair back, swirling it up and fastening it on top of her head without pins, an expedient move born out of years of practice. Sweat poured down her neck, trailed into her clothing, saturated her bra. Her own scent assailed her, unabashedly sexual. What had he thought? That she was some easy mark out for a little vacation fun? God, what had she done? What was it about him . . . ?

She whirled and retreated, ripping clothes off, leaving them where they fell, then stepped into the shower and let the cold, punishing water beat against her, drowning out the messages of guilt and desire, tamping down the impulsiveness she'd spent so much of her life trying not to give in to.

Sliding into a wisp of silk undid everything the cold shower had done. Sensuous fabric abraded nipples that wouldn't unpucker, caressed her abdomen, teased her sensitized thighs as she paced her suite.

So this is passion. Every previous experience not only paled in comparison, but disintegrated into cold ashes. Restless, she moved onto the balcony and surveyed the beach and patio. Her gaze zeroed in on Iain as he sat on the dividing wall. If he'd been a smoker, the red glow of a cigarette would have punctuated the air. Instead, he merely slouched, staring at the ocean, his arms resting on his thighs, hands dangling impotently between his knees.

He looked so alone.

And she was such a sucker for strays.

Three

———

He thought he hadn't remembered correctly, thought he'd glorified her in his mind. But here she was, in the light of day, 7:00 a.m. to be exact, still looking like a fantasy come true. Iain ducked under a wave, came up exhaling, and turned toward the beach to watch Kani stride into the ocean.

He knew what she was feeling—surprise that the water could be so warm this early in the day. It had shocked him a little, too, that it could feel better than a bath. He caught a wave and bodysurfed in until he could pull up directly in front of her as she stood thigh-deep, waiting for the wave to pass.

With both hands, he pushed his hair back and silently assessed her. She gave him look for look.

Finally he smiled. "'Mornin', Average."

Her eyes took on some sparkle. "Hollywood."

"Sleep well?"

There was the slightest hesitation. "Like a baby."

Oh, Kani, you don't lie well, do you? You've got to learn to school your expressions if you want to fool me.

"You're an early bird," he commented.

"It all beckoned, you know?"

"I know. Are you a good swimmer?"

"Pretty good. I spent a few vacations in Hawaii with my grandmother, who taught me to have a healthy respect for the ocean's power. You're a great bodysurfer. I can never seem to really get into a wave. I don't know what I do wrong, but I seem to end up right behind the point I need to be."

"Go out and catch one. I'll watch."

"Okay."

She had gone barely five feet when he whistled. "That's some suit, Average."

Kani hid her blush by diving into a wave. She knew what the bikini looked like, the way the French-cut style displayed her taut dancer's buttocks and thighs, compliments of years of ballet training. Another time, another place, she would have hesitated at wearing the garment. Here, in this exotic vacation wonderland with this obviously attracted man, she was more than willing to wear the revealing suit.

Iain set his hands low on his hips, tipped back his head, and blew out a breath as he moved waist-deep in the water. He seemed destined to stay perpetually aroused around her.

The tail of her braid floated on the surface as she watched the waves, waiting for the right one. Finally one with potential began to crest and she spun around. He watched her take three long pulls, get caught in the frothy foam at the back of the wave, then pull up and slap her open hands onto the water's surface in frustration.

"See? I can't ride it like you do."

He waded toward her. "I'll bet you'll be riding just fine after a couple of lessons."

Kani sputtered at the innuendo and pushed a stream of water at him with the heel of her hand.

He lifted his hands in apparent innocence. "What'd I say? Come on, you know what I meant."

"I most certainly do."

Iain laughed. She was a helluva lot of fun, this Kani Warner. Easy to rile and, he noticed as well, easy to settle down. "C'mere. I'll show you what you're doing wrong."

Kani grasped his outstretched hand and fought the weight of the water to ease up beside him. His hands bracketed her waist.

"Stretch out on your stomach." As she complied, he slid one hand under her, covering her navel and balancing her on his fingers. His other hand cupped her shoulder, forcing her to round it.

Kani turned her head toward him. "I don't suppose you could give me a lesson without touching me."

"I don't suppose," he said with a wry grin.

"I thought not."

"Pay attention now. You have to do three things differently. First, you need to take two or three more strokes than you're taking and get yourself farther into the wave. You hover behind it and never catch its force. Second, you need to round your shoulders and let your arms just hang back, curling your hands under you." They stood up as a wave rolled past them, then he moved in front of her as he continued, his hands supporting her shoulders, her legs kicking slowly to keep herself afloat. "Third, duck your head a little rather than lifting it straight up all the time. Think like a seal. They have perfect bodysurfing form."

"Don't I need to see where I'm going?"

"Lift your head occasionally. You'll see potential hazards soon enough to avoid a crash." His tone was wry. "I don't think you need to worry about it at the moment."

They shared the stretch of ocean in front of the hotel with only two other people riding boogie boards at least a hundred yards away. As she tucked her legs to stand, Kani acknowledged the only slight possibility of crashing headlong into someone. Iain still had his hands on her shoulders as she uncurled upward, and he let his palms slide over her breasts to drift into the water as she rose fully. Her widened eyes reflected her surprise.

"You get near, I'm going to touch," he said calmly as his hardened body pulsed with longing.

Her brows lifted. "Meaning if I can't stand the heat, get out of the kitchen?"

"That's one way of putting it."

She smiled leisurely. "I've always enjoyed cooking."

Delighted, Iain laughed and shoved her gently toward the breakers. "Let's see how good a student you make."

She walked backward, grinning. "Oh, I'm a pretty good student. And an *excellent* teacher."

"So when's class in session, Teach?"

I really must remember not to play word games with him.

"How do you feel about night school?" she queried, breathless.

"Night school, day school, hell, reform school—I don't care. I just like to learn. Look out," he shouted before a wave broke into her, shoving her into him. He caught her around the waist; she clung to his shoulders before lifting both arms around his neck and kicking upward. They were suspended briefly, then she drifted down as the wave receded and her feet touched the sandy bottom. But he was set on teasing her, arousing her utterly, and also maintaining their privacy. He set her away from him. "Go grab a wave, Average."

He sounded disinterested, but Kani had been pulled snugly enough to him to feel how aroused he was. She gloated openly at him, smirked and preened as she backed off. "Yes, master. I hear and obey."

He narrowed his eyes at her. "You have a smart mouth."

She grinned over her shoulder at him, batting her eyes. "Talented, too."

Horrified at her words, Kani kept turning until she faced the horizon. She couldn't believe she'd said that. *What is getting into me?*

Iain MacKenzie, her mind whispered back. *And I think he's going to get into you but good.*

* * *

Kani stood under the outdoor shower next to the pool, rinsing the salt and sand off and admiring Iain's backside as he fixed two cups of coffee from the "first-aid pot" set out for early risers.

"Here's the plan," he said as he handed her a cup. They moved to sit on the concrete wall. "As soon as we're done with our coffee, we'll go to our rooms, shower, change and head out for a walk before it gets too hot. Then we'll have a leisurely breakfast and sack out for a while on some lounges. Okay with you?"

Kani decided it was really rather pleasant having someone else make decisions. "Perfect."

"Did you bring anything to read?"

She smiled, thinking of the romance novels her friend Julia had tossed into her suitcase. "I've got reading material—"

"Hey, *señor,* want to go fishing?"

Iain and Kani looked down at the smiling Mexican man holding up an eight-by-ten glossy color photo of some fishermen standing beside some very large fish.

"No, thanks," Iain said.

"Fish are running good right now, *señor.* Bring in lots of sailfish, some marlin, some tuna. You can bring your wife to watch. No charge."

Kani lifted her brows at Iain. "And you were worried I'd spend too much on vacation, *dear.*"

Iain grinned at her.

"What day do you want to go, *señor?* I got room tomorrow or Friday. Another couple from this hotel is going Friday. You can share the boat."

"I'll think about it."

"I come back later, okay? What's your name, *señor?*"

Iain sighed. "Iain."

The man grinned, his gold-capped tooth winking in the sun. "My name is Ismael. And your pretty wife?"

Kani stretched out her hand. "Kani. You sell lots of trips, *señor?*"

"Lots of trips. Catch lots of fish."

"I don't know much about these kinds of fish, except for tuna, of course. Are they good to eat?"

"Nah. But they are fun to catch. The marlin, she fights. Hooo, does she fight. Sometimes for hours. Sailfish, not so much of a fight. You can have them stuffed and mounted. Shipped home."

Kani laughed. "I don't have a wall large enough to hang one. What if we don't want to take it home?"

"We give it to the orphanage, *señora*."

"To eat? I thought you said they weren't good eating."

"Not to Americans." A grin split his face. "We are not so picky."

Iain settled in comfortably, enjoying listening to the conversation, letting Kani make the small talk.

"You speak English well, Ismael," she said.

He shrugged. "I lived in Minnesota a little while."

"Sounds cold."

"*Sí*, was very cold. My first wife, she was from Minnesota. She came to Mazatlán on vacation. We fell in love but she would not marry me unless I go to Minnesota. So I went. We had a baby, a girl, April. So pretty! She comes three times a year to see me."

"What happened to your marriage?"

"I could not take the cold. So my wife she moved here with me, but she did not like the hot summers. We are good friends now."

"Marriage called due to weather," Iain commented dryly.

Ismael nodded his head philosophically as Kani laughed. "*Sí, señor*. This is true. But I am married again. My wife, she had a baby last night. A boy. I am so happy."

"Oh, Ismael, that's wonderful. How much did he weigh? How big is he?"

"I don't know in American pounds or inches. He is about this big." Ismael held his hands out, way out, and Kani laughed again before pushing his hands closer together.

"You really are a fisherman, aren't you? Did you see him being born?"

"No. I saw my daughter, though. But I have a son! I am so happy! So, *señor,* you want to take a fishing trip on Friday? Forty dollars, American. Fifteen dollar deposit."

"Let me think about it."

"He is a tough man, eh, *señora?*" Ismael teased Kani.

She eyed Iain thoughtfully. "On the outside, I think."

"I come back tomorrow, okay, *señor?* We do business then. *Adiós.*"

"Do you think he's trustworthy?" Iain asked as Ismael stopped to talk with another couple farther down. "He could take the deposit money and run."

Her eyes widened in surprise. "Of course I think he's trustworthy. Are you always so suspicious?"

"Are you always so trusting? I'll bet you've had your illusions shattered a few times."

Her chin came up. "Maybe I have. But I'd still rather believe the best about people. Life's full of pain, Iain. We go on, anyway." She swigged the last of her coffee and decided to change the subject. "Would you like a second cup?"

"Sure, thanks." He passed his empty cup to her, then stopped her from standing. "Don't delude yourself, Kani. Don't look for more from me than I can give. I'm not often gentle."

She wished she could just lean over and press a soft, healing kiss to his lips. Instead, she trailed a finger from his collarbone to his thumb. "I think you're gentle when it counts."

They stepped into the elevator together to go shower and change for their walk. Kani pushed four, and Iain glanced curiously at her.

"I'm on four, too."

Kani digested this information in silence until they began walking down the corridor and he didn't leave her side. "I'm at the end, 4102. Knock on my door when you're ready, if you want. Or I can meet you by the stairs to the beach."

Iain laughed. "I don't believe this. I'm in 4101. We share the common entrance to the double suite." He held up his key and, still chuckling, opened the outer door that led into a small joint entry.

Iain's room was straight ahead, a studio unit with two double beds, refrigerator, bathroom and television. Kani had a suite with a living room, kitchen, two bathrooms and a bedroom. Each unit locked separately.

"I don't understand the arrangement of these rooms," she said as they stood awkwardly in the entry.

"I was curious myself, and asked the bellhop, who couldn't speak English. So I asked the manager last night. He said the two rooms are sold as one unit, but each side could be rented individually. Whoever owns this unit in the time-share wasn't going to use it this year, so each side was rented out separately." He shook his head. "This is rather amazing, isn't it?"

Could Uncle Henry have been matchmaking? Did he set this up? "You don't by chance know Henry Fisher, do you?"

"Henry being the generous Uncle Henry who gave you this trip? No, sorry. Never heard of him. Why don't you knock when you're ready. I'll probably be done before you."

She was still a little numb. He plucked her key from her fingers and opened her door, then stood back, passing her the key as she stepped in front of him.

"Now who's the suspicious one? Do people often play matchmaker for you, Kani?" He grinned at they way she narrowed her eyes at him. "See you shortly."

They wandered as tourists do, picking up shells, people watching, talking about what they saw. Kani noticed how intensely focused Iain could be, whether on her or a shore fisherman or a parasailer, as if he was storing the experience in some computer bank. Iain noticed how easily distracted Kani was, how she could suddenly lose a thought if a child's laugh caught her attention, or shift her mood from serious to gleeful in an instant, how she could be enchanted by a tiny crab scrambling sideways across the sand or an unbroken spiral shell rolling in with the surf.

After the long walk, they enjoyed a leisurely breakfast. Later they slathered on sunscreen and stretched out under the *palapas* with their books.

Iain glanced at the voluptuous woman in the clutches of a tall, dark and handsome man on the cover of Kani's romance. "Let me know when you get to a good part, okay?" he said.

"By 'good,' you mean sexy?"

"Of course."

"But it doesn't have the same impact out of context. You have to get to know the characters first, like them, be anxious for them to make love. Then the 'good' scene means something."

"No. *You* need that. *I* don't."

She almost stuck her tongue out at him. Instead, she pushed up his book so she could read the cover. "Yuk. War stories."

"Not stories," he countered. "Diaries and letters. Real life."

"You don't like fiction?"

"I like fiction. I like fact."

Kani tapped her forefinger against her lips thoughtfully. "I'll bet you like nonfiction best. In fact, I'll bet you've never read anything frivolous in your life."

"You'd be surprised."

"Oh, yeah? Name the last frivolous book you read."

He dropped the book against his stomach as he considered.

"See? You can't even remember!"

"Wait a minute, Average. It'll come to me. Oh, yeah. *How to Pick Up Girls.*"

Kani swatted him with her book, laughing. "And exactly how old were you?"

"Fifteen, sixteen. Hey, I learned a lot. You're sitting next to me, aren't you?" He returned her smile. "Have I told you how beautiful you are?"

She didn't take him seriously. She knew how to accentuate her best features, but she didn't believe for a minute that she was beautiful. Kani angled toward him; she was fairly certain the turquoise eyes behind the dark sunglasses were focused on the flesh plumped up above her bikini top. "I'll bet that's the first line you learned from the book."

Iain shifted leisurely to mirror her. They were each stretched out on their sides, their chairs almost touching. "You knock my socks off."

She hesitated at the serious tone in his voice. "You're not wearing any socks."

"See?"

"Why haven't you kissed me yet?"

Four

———

She clamped her mouth shut, shocked at herself.

Iain stared at her—at least she thought he was staring at her—then he hooked two fingers behind the scrap of fabric between her breasts and tugged her toward him. His mouth hovered an inch from hers as he separated his fingers and pressed one into each breast. "I knew you'd be this firm," he breathed. "God, Kani, you're spectacular. Don't you know that?"

Her breath came in short, soft pants as she shook her head at him.

"I haven't kissed you yet because I don't want to kiss you for the first time in public."

Her sunglasses weren't as dark as his. He could see her eyes widen and her gaze dart side to side as she became aware again of all the people around them. He withdrew his fingers slowly and let her drift back.

Her flesh burned where his fingers had pressed. She flopped onto her back and reopened the book. After half a minute, Iain lifted the book from her hands and turned it right side up.

"Thank you," she said primly. "Aren't you going to read?"

His lips twitched with suppressed laughter. "My book is otherwise occupied at the moment."

Kani glanced at the open book spread facedown across his swim trunks. Her face burned hot. "Oh."

He gave in to the laughter. "You're priceless, Average. You really are."

"Thank you. I think."

"Oh, it was a compliment, all right. About the highest I can give you."

"You confuse me," she admitted after a moment.

He smiled. "Thank you."

"I don't think I intended that as a compliment, Hollywood."

"But I'll take it as one." He lifted his book. "Don't forget to share the good parts."

They read, they napped, they swam, they tanned. They talked with the people around them more than with each other, but their gazes kept returning to ask silent questions and offer equally mute answers.

Their voiceless language spoke volumes.

Kani chose her clothing carefully for the evening. Panties smaller than her bathing suit, sheer silk bra, a pale yellow sleeveless crop top and matching gauze skirt encircled by a bright fabric-and-bead belt she'd bought from a beach vendor that afternoon after a lively bargaining session. Her hair flowed down her back, makeup was applied sparingly, and a light, brisk scent was spritzed in a cloud around her.

Dinner was consumed automatically, the wonderful flavors and textures going untasted and unappreciated. This time when he invited her for a moonless walk, she accepted.

He stopped their descent to the beach by guiding her to sit on a lounge chair and crouching before her to remove her sandals, letting his hand glide up her calf to the back of her knee and trailing back down to catch the heel of each shoe and slide it off.

From his position, he caught the fragrance of her, the essence of arousal, the essence of Kani. He stood abruptly, turning from her slightly as he slid out of his own sandals and kicked them under the chair with hers, tangling them in a bizarre imitation of lovemaking.

She glanced under the chair to see what had captured his intense gaze and was startled to see their shoes ensnared, touching intimately. *They're just shoes! Oh, my, everything seems erotic right now.*

Iain pulled her up and swept a hand down her back, letting his palm settle in that lovely indentation between back and buttocks as he drew her in front of him for a moment. Her eyes widened as she felt his aroused body press against her abdomen. His loose Hawaiian-print shirt covered his blatant response; nothing hid the desire in his eyes.

Kani swallowed hard. "I think we'd better walk."

"Easy for you to say." His tone was wry, but a smile soon followed.

They walked in silence for several minutes, fingers entwined. Iain admired her profile as she lifted her face into the breeze and shook her head, sending her hair rippling and floating in the wind. He'd never been obsessed with hair before, never cared what length or what color it was, whether it was curly or straight. But he was fixated on Kani's hair. When it was wet, he'd thought it much longer, but dry, the curls brushed just below her shoulder blades, the silken length just short enough to occasionally tumble over her shoulders and tease her breasts. Longish bangs feathered her forehead and trailed the sides of her face, ending at her chin, a delicate frame for the lovely oval face.

Kani spent little time analyzing Iain and her incredible reaction to him; she had already accepted that he appealed to her well beyond any other man. The sense of inevitability that had touched her the night before settled like a cloak over her now. She didn't understand why she always ended up with Peter Pan men who couldn't seem to grow up. At least this time she'd have only a week with him; she wouldn't end up supporting him until the right job came along. She wouldn't fall in love with him and have him move on to New York to try theater there, leaving her behind in her continual struggle to save her little theater, only this time without a warm back to curl up against during a cold night.

Because the next time she fell in love, it had to be with someone she could count on to stay with her—no matter what. She wanted her own home, a husband to cherish who cherished her, too, and children to cuddle.

But Iain would go back to Los Angeles and she would return to her life in San Francisco. They would face their demons separately. In the meantime, they could hold those devils at bay for each other.

She'd never thought she'd hear herself say that, never thought she could be so casual about sex. She'd thought she'd been in love with the other men in her life; lovemaking was the next natural step. But she didn't have any illusions about Iain. He was a stranger. One she instinctively trusted, but a stranger nonetheless. And she didn't think she could resist him.

"Hawaii's the only other place I've been to with a climate like this," she said quietly. "It's nine o'clock at night and still warm, even right at the ocean's edge. Is it like this in Southern California?"

"Not really. I've never considered the water there cold, but compared to this, it is."

"Do you spend a lot of time at the beach?"

"I've played volleyball with the same group of guys on Wednesday nights and Sunday mornings for almost ten years. It's really great exercise, then we go out to eat afterward. It's one of the things I look forward to most each week."

He released her hand to slide his arm around her and tuck her close to him. Her short blouse skimmed his knuckles as he cupped the bare skin above her waist and stroked her rhythmically with his thumb. In return, Kani slid her hand under his shirt and massaged his lower back before hooking her fingers into his waistband.

A wave caught them by surprise, dampening her hem and splashing his thighs. They jogged toward a rock wall just past a large, noisy hotel, and he leaned against the boulders in a small, dark crevice and pulled her to him, pressing her head under his chin.

Heaven, she thought as she snuggled. Her fingers toyed with the buttons on his shirt, loosening them until she could spread the fabric and lay her cheek against his bare skin. It felt so good to be held!

Iain's hands wandered with infinite slowness over her, stimulating nerve endings an inch at a time, arousing her with deliberate, unhurried care, until her tongue touched his nipple and stroked once. She tongued a hot, wet trail across his chest, sucking his skin lightly, nibbling; exhaling heated breath against his sensitized skin.

He spun her to face away from him, imprisoned her within his arms, and rubbed his bare chest and stomach against her until tiny streaks of lightning crackled between them. He curved his hands under her blouse to cup her breasts and flicked the catch of her bra. Drawing his hands out, he caught her bra straps, and, with her help, tugged them down her arms, softly pulling the scrap of fabric off her and stuffing it into his back pocket. Grasping the hem of her blouse he then slid the gauzy fabric of her top back and forth, back and forth, across her pebbled breasts until she moaned and tipped her head back.

"Kiss me," she breathed.

He pushed her hair aside and pressed his lips to her neck, his hands creeping under her blouse to once again cup her breasts and thumb her hard nipples. Tightening his arms around her waist, he spooned her to him...and noticed another couple walking near the water's edge.

His voice was so quiet it was almost a whisper. "Anyone intent on dazzling someone can do it, especially if there's a sexual attraction to begin with. We are vulnerable so many times in our lives, often for just brief moments. Maybe we've had an argument with someone we care about, and maybe it's a problem that wouldn't normally last beyond a few days, but someone comes along at the exact instant we're vulnerable, and instead of settling things with the one we care about, we find it easier to turn to someone new. Or maybe we're just lonely. The reasons are endless."

Iain had turned villains into heroes on the daytime serial enough times to know how it could be managed with the right words and a competent actor. He was afraid that this week he was becoming someone she would want rather than someone she could care for beyond the physical. He wanted to show her who he was. He *was* different with her, gentler, in many ways more open. Had he been plotting her seduction all along, as he would a script? He was afraid of the answer, but he was damn well going to give her an out.

"You're vulnerable for some reason right now. I don't know why. But whether we take our relationship further has to be your decision, Kani. You have to live with it."

"So do you," she whispered.

"You're different from me. I can, and I have, made love and never looked back."

"That's not making love."

"Had sex then, if the semantics are important to you. We have less than a week before we return home to our individual problems. We can make each other forget for now. But what about at home? This isn't *Same Time, Next Year.* Nobody's written scenes for us. I don't want you to have any regrets."

She turned in his arms. "Why are you warning me? Why is this only my decision?"

He threaded her hair with his fingers. "Because I don't want you hurt. Because I think you've been hurt enough. Because I'm not usually the man you think you've come to know."

"Do you beat women?"

"No! But cruelty comes in many forms—indifference, insensitivity."

Her opinion of him underwent an abrupt turnabout. This was no Peter Pan. This was a good, strong, mature man who'd had some bad breaks, that was all. What man who considered himself cruel would warn her, would give her the chance to acknowledge the attraction and yet turn from it without blaming her?

She lifted her hands to his face. "I want you. This. Everything."

"I'm afraid..."

"Of what? Tell me."

"Of how good it's going to be. Of how we won't be able to let go of the memories. This isn't real life. It's no measure of how we would get along away from some exotic environment. I'm afraid you'll think yourself in love with me. And I'll only hurt you."

"You won't hurt me. My eyes are open, Iain. Wide open."

"God, Kani, I'm trying to be gentle. You make me want to be gentle."

"And you make me want to be reckless. So who wins, Hollywood? Who wins?"

He tightened his hold and dragged her closer, bending his head. "Last chance."

She shook her head, her hair performing a silken dance over his arms. The gold dust in her eyes reflected the stars. "Not last chance, Iain. First choice. Only choice."

He groaned as he took her mouth, giving in, letting loose, drawing her in, shedding his restraints. *I'm exploding, and I can't stop it.*

Oh, my, this man can kiss. Like everything else he did, he stayed focused on just the one task—on her mouth, her lips and tongue and teeth. They kissed and kissed, one overpowering, compelling kiss after another, more than she'd ever kissed anyone at one sitting before moving to the next step. And with each kiss she grew a little more drugged, a little more entranced, a little more hungry.

"Your room or mine?" he breathed against her mouth.

"I don't care."

"Do you want to freshen up first, or change?"

She sucked in a breath as his fingers glided over her buttocks and he moved against her. "It's not like it's our honeymoon or anything. I like feeling it's spontaneous."

In the deepest recesses of his mind, he acknowledged he wanted this to be like a wedding night for her, with champagne and candlelight—a white lacy gown for her, silk pajama bottoms for him. An image of himself carrying her across a threshold branded itself in his mind and wouldn't be shaken loose. For all the cautions he'd given her, it was he who was in danger of taking this week too seriously. *So what are you going to do about it, man?*

"On second thought," he heard her say, "maybe my room would be best. I have some, uh, boxes of, you know."

He pulled his head back and looked down at her. "I'll be damned."

"I'm on the Pill, but—"

"You don't take chances," he said, completing the sentence. "Neither do I, Kani."

"Good. And as for the other...I didn't exactly pack them. My friend did. As a joke."

He moved away, smiling. "How many?"

"Twenty-four."

"Wow."

"She was very hopeful."

He brushed her hair from her face. "An indisputable scorekeeper. There'll be no question how many times we..."

At his hesitation, Kani filled in the blank. "...had sex."

Made love, his mind screamed. Made love. "Yeah," he said flatly. "Had sex."

"I'm getting real tired of just talking about it."

He smiled and grabbed her hand before jogging down the beach, shortening his normal stride until she matched him. They flew across the sand and raced up the stairs, pausing only to wash off their feet under the low faucet and pick up their sandals before they race-walked to the elevator.

When the doors slid shut, Iain propelled her against the back wall and attacked her mouth with his until the doors whooshed open. Without lifting his mouth, he backed them out of the elevator, then leaned her against the nearest wall and drove his tongue into her, savoring the taste of her heated passion.

"I've never been kissed before," she breathed as he lifted his head.

Iain was stunned. "You're a—?"

"Virgin? No. Does that disappoint you?"

"Hell, no. But what do you mean?"

"I mean if that's what kissing really is, I've never been kissed before. No one has ever made me feel like that with a kiss."

"Like what?"

"Like my mouth was connected to my womb by some kind of power source. I feel electrocuted."

Don't say that, Kani. Oh, God, don't say things like that to me. "Kani," he whispered, as he touched his lips lightly to hers. He felt cold metal touch his hand and realized she was pressing her room key into his palm.

Then suddenly they were in her softly lit bedroom. Iain folded the bedding back to the bottom sheet; Kani turned from him to retrieve one of the boxes from the built-in dresser. As she closed the drawer, she felt his heated body press the length of hers. She raised her head to watch him in the mirror, watched him lift the box from her hand and toss it onto the bed, watched him grasp the hem of her crop top and peel it over her head. Watched his tanned hands mold her shoulders, drift down her arms, move across her stomach and glide up to cup the glorious weight of her breasts, their whiteness gleaming against his darker skin.

She closed her eyes and leaned back into him.

"Watch," he urged, and didn't begin caressing her anew until she opened her eyes and lowered her gaze. He didn't touch her nipples for the longest time, not until they couldn't harden further. Even then his fingers merely skimmed the tight, sensitive flesh. She lifted her arms to twine around his neck and saw him react to how her breasts changed shape with the movement. They watched each other in the mirror, her hair a sultry cloud between them. "Keep looking," he said, turning them sideways and bending to kiss her shoulder. She watched his tongue draw rivers across her skin, circle her dusky nipple and suck it deeply into his mouth. His fingers worked the fastening on her belt, and it soon dropped to the floor. Her skirt pooled at her feet, and he knelt in the billowing fabric and pressed his face against her stomach. Then he curved his hands into her panties and slid them down and off, following their descent with his lips. When he wove his way back up her body, he stopped to taste her damp heat and reveled in her involuntary jerk against him as his mouth settled intimately on her.

She grasped his shirt to pull him up and immediately stripped the garment from him. "Watch," she ordered. Spinning him to face the mirror, she stepped behind him to unzip his shorts and push them down. He was wearing some sort of pouch underwear, the kind she'd only seen in mail order catalogs, and, fascinated, she took a moment just to observe him before sliding her fingertips under the elastic waistband and bringing the fabric down his body. He murmured her name as he watched her splay her fingers and flatten her hands on his hipbones, then move to grasp and encircle him. "Keep watching," she urged as she turned them sideways and knelt before him.

"It's too much," he groaned, pulling her back up.

Then they were kneeling on the bed, four anxious hands applying the contents of a packet.

She watched him try to restrain himself, saw him take calming breaths. "Don't, Iain. Give me everything. Don't hold back. I'm more than ready. I can take it."

He searched her face—the wild mane of hair tumbling gloriously around her, the eyes which mirrored his passion perfectly, the kiss-swollen lips, parted and tempting. His gaze swept down, caressing her perfect breasts with their alluring crests, following the flat, firm abdomen to the cluster of dark curls, admiring the toned muscles and smooth skin.

He desired more than just the body. It came to him not in a flash of lightning but in the glow of starlight that once he made love to this woman—and it *would* be making love—he couldn't go back to being the man he had been.

"Are you sure?" he asked, because *he* wasn't.

And in that instant Kani Warner fell in love with Iain MacKenzie, with the man who put her first, beyond his own needs. With the man who offered more than he expected in return. With the man who hadn't yet learned to love himself and, therefore, to give love.

From her kneeling position, she arched back slowly, lifting her arms to him, offering her body. He lowered himself to her, reluctantly, hungrily, almost beyond sanity.

She sighed as she felt the emanating heat of his hard body cover hers. "This is inevitable, Iain."

He groaned her name as he sheathed himself in her welcoming warmth. His body stiffened; he was seconds away from climax already. But he held himself almost motionless, grinding against her only enough to send her into the vortex as he kissed her deeply, using his tongue as he would use his body. She made a low, urgent sound deep in her throat and her slick heat tightened around him even as her legs did. Only then did he drive into her, giving in to the incredible passion she both offered and drew.

He should say something. He knew he should say something, but everything that filtered through his mind sounded trite, and he'd never been one for commentary after the act. He settled for rising up on his arms a little and examining her face.

She opened her eyes halfway, drew in a deep breath, and smiled as she exhaled, as content as any woman can be who'd found herself in love with a man determined not to love anyone, a man who would walk away if he'd had the slightest inkling of her feelings. "Umm."

He smiled in return. "I take it I passed the test, Teach."

"I'd say you're definitely above average."

He reversed their positions in an unhurried motion, and she stretched out on him, resting her chin on her arms, which were crossed and balanced on his chest.

"Looks like now I'm *below* Average," he remarked.

She laughed. "You're very clever with words."

"You're very clever yourself." His hands made long, sweeping motions down her back, massaging her muscles. "I need to get up for a minute."

She sat up quickly, swung a leg over him and bounced into the bathroom. "I'll take care of it," she said over her shoulder and quickly returned with tissues and a warm, wet washcloth.

Iain lay speechless at the way she gave so openly and naturally of herself. It didn't seem to matter that he hadn't curled up and spent a half hour talking. Yet that was what he wanted to do. *Guess I'm going to be paid back in spades,* he thought in rueful reflection. *Kani is the revenge of every other woman I've made love to—*had sex with—*then treated with blasé disregard.*

"Care to join me in a shower?" she asked as she swept her hair into a knot on top of her head.

"You work out with weights, don't you?" He watched her arm muscles flex and was mesmerized by the way her breasts moved as she made quick work of her mane of hair.

"My brother forced me into it ten years ago, when I was eighteen. Now it's just habit and, of course, part of the social life of a big-city single woman, something I imagine you're familiar with." *And it was all worth it to see that admiring look in your eyes.* "Come on."

Kani dropped a bit of silk over her head after the mutually pleasurable shower they shared. The nearly transparent pale blue gown scooped low over her breasts. The hem ended high on her thighs and would offer a tantalizing view when she sat. She dangled his underwear toward him.

"Put these on again. I want to scrutinize this fashion statement a little more," she told him, then circled him to inspect the pouch and elastic waistband once he had. "Is it comfortable?"

"Normally. When you're not looking at me like that. It's getting a little snug under inspection."

"I do admire the fit, Hollywood. You certainly do fill it out."

"I think that's your doing, Average."

She grinned, pleased. He was the easiest man she'd ever been naked around and, at the same time, the most intoxicating. She felt not a moment's discomfort or hesitance at him observing her nude body, and yet she also found she couldn't drift back down fully from arousal. "I never travel without peanut butter and crackers. Want some?"

"All of a sudden, I'm hungry," he said with a smile. He followed her out the door and into the combination kitchen, dining area and living room. "How'd you rate such a big place? I've only got a studio."

"I don't know." She put crackers on a plate, opened the jar of peanut butter, and grabbed two knives. "I bought soda and beer at the little grocery store across the street. What's your pleasure?"

He cringed. "Soda, I guess."

She placed everything on the coffee table, then dropped onto the sofa. Iain was standing at the open door to the balcony, admiring the view. "No one can see in here. Quite an advantage facing the ocean." He turned and eyed her speculatively. "Nice to know we'll have freedom wherever we are in the suite."

She held up a cracker already spread with peanut butter, and he sat beside her as he accepted it and took a bite. Her feet were flat on the ground, her legs together. *Lean back, love.*

Kani leaned back to savor the snack and caught him staring at her with hungry eyes. As his gaze traveled up her body and settled on her face, she licked the peanut butter off the cracker with a long, smooth stroke of her tongue. *This isn't me,* she thought wildly. *Oh, yes, it is. This is you, finally, with the right man.*

Iain tossed the remains of his cracker back onto the plate, swigged some soda to dampen his mouth, and then grimaced at the combination of tastes, reaching for Kani. "You're one helluva sexy piece of work, Average."

"I thought you wanted to eat."

His scorching look made her snap her mouth shut. Never taking his gaze off hers, he peeled her gown over her head. Lips to lips, body to body, he urged her flat. His mouth wandered on a journey of discovery, finding peaks and valleys, a barren plain and a small, neat forest guarding a fragrant glen.

"I feel like a sacrifice," she said breathlessly. "Are you sure no one can see in? All the lights are on."

"Impossible to see in. Just be quiet and enjoy it."

He felt her give herself up to him, but not before she uttered a few more words. "Do I really have to be quiet?"

He shifted, closed the sliding glass doors, then focused all of his attention on pleasing her. "Feel free to make all the noise you want, Average."

She did.

Five

As Kani drifted into consciousness at sunrise, she realized she'd never awakened in a man's arms before. In the same bed, yes. But never in his arms.

Her cheek lay against his chest, her ear pillowed on the muscle and flesh where chest drifted into collarbone. His heart thumped steadily; his breath danced rhythmically in and out, in and out; gentle, reassuring, constant. His skin breathed the tang of sweat and ocean, not an unpleasant combination, mingled with her own scent. She committed it to memory.

"What are you thinking about, so quiet and intent?"

His morning voice rumbled from his chest and echoed in her ear. She blinked back sudden tears at the intimacy in his tone and tried to keep her answer light.

"I wake up glued to you after a night like we had, and you have to ask?"

Iain tightened his hold and drew her over him to enfold her solidly within his arms. His legs imprisoned hers within upraised knees. "It was an incredible night," he said quietly, surely. He had recognized early that some of what they'd done last night had been new to her, had wondered briefly about the fools she'd dated before, and then had made a conscious decision to comply with her request that he not hold back. If she'd been uncomfortable or unsure about anything, it hadn't lasted beyond a moment of surprised consideration. He'd found her lack of guile amazingly sexy, her near innocence—and he was sure she'd slug him if he called her innocent to her face—intriguing.

"Want to do a little bodysurfing?" he queried after several minutes had passed.

Maybe some body slamming, she thought brazenly. The night had been a revelation, and she needed time to think about all that had happened, physically and emotionally.

She'd never realized how much one could discover about a person while making love. But sometime during the night, it had struck her that a man who was selfish in bed, who cared more about his own pleasure than hers, was bound to be selfish out of bed. Why hadn't she ever seen that before? It would have spared her an unbelievable amount of grief.

And Iain MacKenzie was a generous man.

"Kani? Are you okay?"

"Yes. Just lazy. Bodysurfing sounds so...energetic."

"Do you want to go back to sleep? I could leave—"

"No! No. Don't go." Her fingers curved into his shoulders and tightened almost painfully.

He murmured soothing little sounds, offered comfort with stroking hands. "I can't read your mind, Kani. You'll have to tell me what you want."

You. Every square inch of you, inside and out. "A swim would be nice," she said as she rolled off him and sprang to her feet.

Iain watched a flicker of unidentifiable emotions cross her face. Was she embarrassed? He swung his legs over the side of the bed to stand beside her. "What's wrong?"

"Nothing," she said quickly. Too quickly.

"Why are you suddenly so uncomfortable with me?"

Because I want to make love again this instant. Because I want to tell you I love you! And it's the last thing you want to hear. She shrugged. "You know, morning-after jitters. Did I do all right? That sort of thing."

"I can't believe you'd doubt it for a minute." He scrutinized every movement of her face. "Do I look like a man not pleased?"

She spun from him and grabbed her hairbrush. "Oh, don't mind me. I'm just tired, I guess."

He observed her struggling with tangles and lifted the brush out of her hand, turning her back to him. Looking over her shoulder into the mirror, he could see her eyes close as he worked the knots from her hair, could see her nipples tighten bit by bit.

"Does this feel good?" he whispered low. At the involuntary sound she made, he stroked the brush through her hair again and again, eventually trailing it gently onto her chest, between her breasts, across her stomach and down her silky abdomen....

Bodysurfing was just going to have to wait.

Kani floated a little past the breakers. She'd caught a few waves, staying right beside him all the way in, then had left him to spend time thinking.

He was unemployed, so he could move. To San Francisco. To be with her. It would be as easy—or as difficult— to find a job in San Francisco as in Los Angeles. She didn't even know what kind of work he did. Hollywood. Maybe television, or the movies. No! Please, no. Don't let him be another fickle performer who believed his destiny lay in L.A. or New York.

Something smooth bumped her flesh and she shrieked, flailing her arms and legs to scare off the creature. Iain came up laughing beside her, and she splashed him wildly.

"You creep! You scared the living daylights out of me." Shakily she treaded water beside him.

"You looked far too comfortable."

Her chin came up. "And I was just about to ask you to move in with me. Now I don't know."

He was silent for a minute as he considered her words. "Move in with you?"

She watched four pelicans glide in formation over them, investigating the fish population their radar eyes could see from twenty feet above the ocean's surface. "I didn't like having you leave this morning to shave and change," she admitted.

Iain hadn't lived with anyone since moving out of his father's apartment fourteen years ago. The most time he'd ever spent with a woman had been a weekend. Part of him wanted the escape route of his own place if he needed it. If he moved his stuff into her suite, it would take time to move out. If he left everything behind, he could leave in an instant if necessary.

And yet, and yet, he didn't want to lose a moment with her. Five days lay between them and their return to real life, real problems. His were enormous, there was no question of that. Too big to get someone else involved in his life right now. And hers? She seemed so uncomplicated. How big could her problems be?

"Okay," he said.

"Just like that? No contingencies?"

He hooked her bathing-suit top and pulled her to him. Their arms and legs tangled as they kept themselves afloat. "One. That when the mood to...have sex strikes you, you'll say so or do something about it. You won't wait for me to instigate it, as you did this morning."

"I didn't—"

His brows lifted. "Didn't you?"

Kani shifted her gaze away from him, puffed up her cheeks, then blew out a long, slow breath. "I suppose maybe you've guessed I'm not as experienced as I may have let on."

Iain hesitated. If he said yes, she'd probably take it as a reflection on her performance. And she was nothing short of perfect, her obvious enthusiasm at pleasing him more than making up for any lack of technique. What she had offered him was honest and genuine; she had given unselfishly, and taken with care. On the other hand, if he said no, she would know he was lying.

"I was flattered, Average, that you wanted me that much." He saw relief in her eyes as she focused on him again. "You taught me a few things, too. I don't want restrictions or barriers between us."

It was all the permission Kani needed. From that moment on she gave him everything of herself, everything except the problem she had to return to and the feelings of failure she'd tried to pack away with her suitcase. Their promise to each other to avoid harsh realities hovered like a specter, occasionally drifting to cloud over their heads, but easily dispatched with a laugh or kiss.

The week passed, sometimes like a jet ski at full throttle, accelerating with desire, skimming over blossoming emotion. The time spent away from each other amounted to the equivalent of waiting for an order at a fast-food restaurant. Kani felt certain he would want to continue the relationship, but she was determined to let him be the one to bring it up. Everything she said or did indicated her willingness to go beyond just the one week.

Beneath a *palapa,* Kani lay curled on her side watching Iain read a section of the book she'd passed on to him, a *good* part. He moved her bookmark back into place, closed the book, and handed it to her.

"We haven't tried that," he remarked. "Want to?"

"Nah. Having sex with waves washing over us sounds entirely too sandy. And public. One of those things that seems exciting when you read about it but wouldn't be comfortable in practice."

Iain's gaze encompassed her whole body. He could remember sitting in these very same seats just a few days ago, eyeing her breasts rounded above her skimpy bikini top and wondering what she'd look like without the suit.

Now he knew. He knew her tan lines, had traced them with his tongue. He knew how her nipples tasted, knew how she liked them drawn deeply into his mouth and rolled between tongue and roof. He knew how her hipbones jutted into soft points under taut skin, how sensitive her skin was high on the inside of her thighs, how she loved to have her hair brushed and her body stroked. He knew how flexible she was, and how strong. How she could make him forget everything.

They had rarely left the resort, venturing out only to do a little window shopping and to make the requisite visit to Señor Frog's, the local hot spot, where they danced on tables to ridiculously loud music and signed their names on the ceiling. She'd worn a snug little minidress, and he'd spent most of the time fantasizing about removing it.

He was quiet for a long time; Kani was content to let him look and remember. "That's quite a knack you have," she said finally, breaking into his reverie.

"What's that?"

"The way you can compliment me silently with your eyes, even behind sunglasses, more than any other man has done with words."

"Foolish other men."

She fiddled with her book. "I suppose you're used to compliments yourself."

"I don't put much store in them. Words are easy."

"I guess I like the words, too."

"One of the differences in the genders," he said with a shrug, trying to avoid a deeper conversation.

Kani took a sudden interest in their surroundings. "You know, the day I got here and realized this was not a place singles would generally go to, I was a little miffed at Uncle Henry for sending me someplace I couldn't find men to flirt with, or even other single women to do some exploring with. Now I'm grateful he chose this place. I haven't had to worry about competition."

"You wouldn't have, anyway. I was hooked from the moment I saw you slink your way out of the ocean."

"Slink?" She laughed.

"Swayed, teased, enticed."

"Is that what I did? Are you saying it was lust at first sight?"

"Yes."

Kani held her breath. "Then why didn't you attempt to sleep with me the first night? You must have known from my reaction that I wouldn't have taken much convincing."

"I don't know. You were different."

"Different from the usual type of woman you date?"

"Yes."

She wished he would elaborate. "We wasted a whole night."

"I was sorry afterward, if that makes you feel any better."

"Tonight's our last night." There. She'd said what they had both avoided saying all day.

He remained silent, just closed a hand over one of hers and squeezed.

"I don't want it to end," she whispered.

He squeezed harder.

"I've fallen—"

His hand covered her mouth. "Don't. Don't say it. I told you. Dammit, I told you." He released her and sat up. "I've got some things to do. I'll see you in a couple of hours."

Then he was gone and Kani stared blindly at the ocean, chastising herself for being weak, hoping desperately that he wasn't in the room moving his things out, wishing she could take the impetuous words back. *He told you the ground rules and you accepted them. Don't make him regret the week. Make him remember it enough that given a little time he'll come to you on his own.* Yes, that was the way to do it. Give him unconditional love and plenty of space. That's the way to deal with Iain MacKenzie.

A note was tucked between the doorknob and the doorjamb of her room. Kani's heart plummeted. Her footsteps slowed, then dragged. She reached for the paper with just her fingertips as if it would burn her. Her heart pounded relentlessly against her chest and it became hard to breathe.

No! No, no, no. I take it back, Iain. I take it back. I need this night with you. Please, please. I need you.

She squeezed her eyes shut as she rubbed the folded paper open with her thumb and forefinger. Opening her eyes to a squint, she focused on the words: "Kani, on the bed is a gift for you." Dammit. Dammit, dammit, *dammit*. A farewell present, like some eighteenth-century British aristocrat buying off his latest ladybird before installing a replacement in his love nest.

"Please wear it tonight and come to my room at seven o'clock. Iain."

Wait a minute. That didn't sound too bad. No longer feeling the need to call for CPR, Kani pushed open her door and went immediately into the bedroom. On the bed lay a beautiful white nightgown and peignoir of sheer soft silk. She smiled as she held the gown up and danced around the room with it, humming and swirling, and ever so grateful.

She had two hours to kill, and she spent most of the time packing, to avoid the inevitable tomorrow. At seven precisely, she knocked on his door.

He was wearing black silk pajama bottoms and he looked like sin—like a hot-fudge sundae must appear to a lifetime member of Weight Watchers. His beautiful sun-streaked hair fell soft and clean away from his forehead, and she loved the way it curled down his neck. His stunning turquoise eyes glittered as he admired her in the gown he had chosen. His mouth tightened against words and his breathing deepened, as if he'd been exercising.

"I'm sorry," she blurted out, her hands outstretched, supplicating.

"Shhh." He grasped both her hands and pulled her into his arms, bending instantly to kiss her, long and hard and passionately. Then he tucked her beneath his chin and held her close, breathing in her fragrance, loving the feel of her in his arms, against his skin, in his heart.

"You're just in time to watch the sunset," he said quietly, moving back and picking up two glasses of champagne he had just poured. "Here, have one. Let's go out onto the balcony."

For the first time, she noticed the room—fresh exotic flowers floating in a low dish on the dining table, which was set for two, covered dishes waiting on a rolling tray cart. Candles were everywhere. The bed was turned down. A scene set for romance. Not just passion...romance. A night to remember. It was important to him, too, she realized. Her head dropped as tears coated her eyes and tightened her throat. *Love and space,* she reminded herself.

She slid her hand into his and walked with him onto the balcony. She lifted her champagne flute. "To Mexican sunsets."

"To fairy godmothers," he added. "And uncles."

They toasted, sipped, and stared into each other's eyes. He encircled her waist with his arm and settled her in front of him as they watched the sun sizzle and the hues deepen, watercoloring a layer of cloud blowing in with reds and pinks and purples.

"Come," he said quietly. He held her chair and seated her in silence, serving them a lovely dinner of chicken and rice, with fresh vegetables, followed by a rich, deep chocolate cake.

They danced without music. The wind picked up dramatically, making the candles flicker and flare, bouncing erratic shadows around the room. When the wind turned cold, he closed the glass doors, cocooning them. As he bent to kiss her, lightning brightened the sky, making him pause to tell her without words that she'd brought light to his life, even as she'd also brought a turbulent storm.

He seduced her while dancing, peeling off her peignoir as they spun around and around, letting it float over the spare bed, like an invitation to a bridegroom, the transparent sleeves outstretched, soliciting.

Thunder. Lightning. Torrents of rain. They absorbed it all, let it guide their emotions, fill their bodies, swell their hearts. He lifted her into his arms and carried her to the bed, laying her down gently, immediately stretching out beside her. Every time her lips parted to speak he covered them with his, stopping words, preventing promises, keeping secrets.

Amid a lightning-and-thunder show that astonished them, he worshiped her as if she were an untouched bride, with reverence and care and tenderness.

"This is cruel," she whispered painfully, finally aware that this was his way of not only saying goodbye but apologizing for the anguish to come. It was then that she knew she'd been wrong to hope for more from him, wrong to think she could make a difference in his life in less than a week.

He didn't brush away her tears, didn't flinch when her nails dug into him, didn't hush her as she climaxed on a sob, intensely, agonizingly, amid blinding flashes of jagged light and the deafening boom of cymbals clashing. He took his punishment, felt her whole body shake as she cried beneath him, and poured himself into her as she locked him relentlessly to her.

Nobility stinks. The words echoed in the deep well of guilt and loss that was Iain's body. She hadn't stopped crying, although she'd tried and tried; tears still flowed silently, accusingly, down her face. His mind reeled. *I have nothing to offer you! No job, no money, nothing. Please, don't make this harder on me.*

Pushing away from him, she sat up, wiping her face and sniffling, not bothering to wrap herself in dignity. "At some point this week, I stopped thinking of what we were doing as 'having sex' and started thinking we were making love. My mistake. I won't make you feel guilty about it any longer. You warned me you could be cruel, and I said I was going into this with my eyes open. Well, they were, but somehow stars flew into them and the whole world sparkled, blinding me to what was real." *I'm just not a lovable person.* "I think I'll go to my room." *Cry my heart out in private,* she added silently as she moved off the bed and slid into her nightgown.

The sorrow reflected in her eyes devastated him, but he didn't try to stop her. He didn't say a word, didn't make a move. She picked up the small cardboard box on the bedside table and counted the condoms inside. Drawing from deep within herself, she dangled the box from her fingertips and offered her best Mae West imitation as she spilled the contents into his lap. "Lucky you. You've still got three more chances tonight, sweet cakes. Or maybe I should keep 'em as a memento. You know what they say. A hard man is good to find." Kani choked on a sob. "But good men are impossible. Goodbye, Iain MacKenzie. I wish you luck in your lonely life."

The door slammed behind her. Iain scattered the packets with a sweeping blow of his arm. Pillows were heaved against the wall, candles extinguished between dry fingers, burning him deeply. He fell across the bed, burying his face in the sheets to inhale the lingering scent of her. *Even when I try to do the right thing, I mess up. God, when will I ever learn?*

He'd let her shatter his defenses, burrow her cheerful way through the shell of cynicism he needed and felt comfortable with. For ten years—ever since he'd learned his mother hadn't died but had abandoned him when he was six years old to a life of dreary existence with his bitter father—he had observed the world with a different eye.

Love died. He'd seen it happen in every relationship around him. And it was the children who suffered, the children who paid. Always.

The storm raged on, within and without, and life as he knew it came to an end. He'd been wrong to think he could resist her as easily as he had every other woman he'd known, and wrong to think he had nothing more to lose. He'd had his heart—now even that was gone.

He lay in the darkness, ignoring the way his soul cried her name until it was hoarse with pain, demanding the shell harden once again.

Six

"Kani, you look so tanned! How I envy you."

Kani allowed herself to be hugged by her friend Julia Linnell and made every effort to appear normal. "You know how easily I tan. I could have gotten this in my backyard."

"But you didn't." They walked out of the international terminal to where Wes waited with their baby, Jeremy, in the car. "So, was it wonderful?"

"It was okay."

Julia stopped her with a hand on her arm. "What's wrong? Are you sick? Montezuma's revenge?"

"Somebody's revenge," she muttered as she passed her suitcase to Wes and ignored the frown on his face. "Hi, Wes. Thanks for picking me up."

"No problem. Jeremy's teething and he's been fussy. He sleeps well in the car." He gave Julia a look of puzzlement, and she shrugged. "Difficult flight?"

Kani opened her mouth, then clamped it shut before she somehow confessed, "I'll be darned if I know. I boarded, ve flew, we landed, I deplaned, I went through customs. I hink I went through customs." Her gaze was frantic. "They vouldn't have let me out if I hadn't, would they?"

"I'm sure you must have," Julia soothed as Wes guided Kani into the back seat next to the sleeping baby.

They drove in silence for several minutes. Kani neither noticed nor cared. Bewildered, Julia and Wes exchanged silent marital shorthand. "So, what'd you do in Mazatlán?" Julia asked.

Kani stared blindly at the passing scenery. "Oh, the usual. Swam, ate, built sand castles, walked along the beach, collected shells, fell in love, had my heart broken."

"Oh!" Julia glanced first at her husband in alarm, then stretched her hand out to her friend. "I'm sorry, Kani."

"Yeah, me, too."

"Want to talk about it?"

"There's not much to say. I was as naive as usual, tried to turn a man into something he isn't, something he isn't even capable of being. At least this time, instead of getting unceremoniously dumped, I got dumped with extraordinary ceremony. I'm telling you, the man should write scripts. He sure knows how to set a scene. Oh, well, the good news is that I'm getting dumped by a higher caliber of male these days. Iain was straight with me from the beginning."

Julia and Wes had exchanged guilty looks as Kani spoke. "In what way?" Julia asked.

"He told me right up front that he wasn't a long-term kind of guy. I thought I could change his mind."

"What was he like?"

"Attractive, intelligent, gentle, sexy. Lonely."

"Lonely?" Wes repeated.

"Yeah. Like he was used to being alone. Didn't quite know what to do with me for a whole week." She expelled a self-deprecating little laugh. "Well, he knew what to *do* with me, just not... Oh, you know what I mean. I think I wanted a knight in shining armor. He was there and attentive, and in my mind I guess I set him on a white charger.

Trouble is, he never takes off his armor, just keeps it welded to his body so that no one can hurt him."

"Sounds like he should have kept his lance to himself," Wes said, angry at his friend Iain, but more angry at himself and Julia for being responsible for Kani's pain.

Kani laughed briefly. "There had to be *some* fringe benefits, Wes. And, Julia, thank you so much for the new clothes. I was stunned."

"I wish you'd had someone more worthy to wear them for."

"He was worthy. He just didn't know it. I feel sorry for him."

"That's generous of you," Julia said. "I think I'd shoot him."

As they came to a stop at Kani's house, she felt the tension in her give way to pain, and fought it. "Do you want to come in?"

Wes shook his head. "We should get Jeremy to bed, but I'll help carry your luggage first. Before you get out though, Julia and I want to touch base with you on something. We've been talking about ways to market Ramshackle Theater to bring in more audiences. We think we might have a solution, but we need to check a few things out first."

"My lease is up in four months, and with the economy the way it is, I don't see recovery in time to save the theater. The arts are the first to slide and the last to recover in a weak economy, you know that. All I want now is to end with a success. I'm tired. I'm tired of being the eternal optimist, tired of putting on a happy face, tired of keeping everyone else's spirits bolstered. Just plain tired. I don't have the energy or the desire to go on.

"Listen, thank you both so much for taking care of Gypsy for me and for dropping her off here before you came to the airport." She stepped out onto the sidewalk and glanced at her house, torn between wishing her brother Bryan were there and being grateful he was out of town for another week. She could never hide anything from Bryan; his eyes pierced straight into her soul.

Julia's look of sympathy made Kani's eyes brighten with tears.

"I'll be all right, Julia. Don't worry about me." But Kani didn't fight the hug that Julia gave her or the sympathetic brush of Wes's hand down her braid. It was good to be home where people loved and appreciated her, where people didn't tamper with her emotions, where scar tissue could form around her heart yet again. Why did that seem like such an impossible task this time?

Julia and Wes stood in silence, watching her move slowly into her house and pull the door quietly shut behind her.

"Well, that didn't go exactly as planned, did it?" Julia said at last.

"We were stupid," Wes agreed.

"Egotistical."

"Omnipotent. Now what?"

"I think you should call Iain and see what his reaction to the week is. Then we'll decide. I never dreamed..." Julia swallowed hard.

"I know, sweetheart. Maybe we can still salvage it."

"I wonder if we should even try, Wes. We've already caused enough pain. What if we just make things worse for her? For them both."

He squeezed his wife's hand. "What if we can make it better?"

Three days passed. Three mornings of working out her frustrations at the gym, along with three shifts at work. The routine was good, settling, Kani decided as she plucked a feather duster from below the bar and began dusting bottles.

Now if she could just do something about the nights...and her dreams. She saw his face, reran the film of their time together in her head to watch his intensity, the way he zeroed in on something that interested him until he was done storing the information. He'd watched families, watched them interact. He'd frowned when parents criticized their children or when children had talked back to their parents, smiled when a family enjoyed themselves or played together. He hungered for a connection of some kind, a family—Kani somehow knew it—one far different from his own.

Are you thinking of me, too, Iain? Are you hurting, or have you put me out of your mind as easily as you thought you could?

"A drill sergeant could use white gloves on those bottles," fellow bartender Jake Bradshaw commented.

Kani smiled at the bar's watchdog—sixty-two years old, five foot five and a wiry one hundred and twenty pounds, Jake had long ago substituted his staff for a nonexistent family. Although the day shift didn't run into as many drunks as the night shift did, he made sure no one stepped over the line with his "girls"—especially with his surrogate daughter, Kani.

"You okay, chickadee?" he asked her, about as personal a question as he would ever ask.

"Hanging in there," she replied before he nodded and moved away. It was comforting just having him near. She caught sight of Wes walking the length of the lounge and she smiled. Everyone was concerned about her, and they seemed to be taking turns making contact, keeping her out of the doldrums.

He plopped a large, heavy envelope on the bar. "Read this," he ordered, tapping it with his finger.

"Hi to you, too, Wes. What is it?"

"Ramshackle's glorious finish."

"A script? Fabulous. Who wrote it?"

"I can't tell you who wrote it because I don't want that to influence you," he said.

"Why would that influence me? Is it someone I know?" Kani pressed. "Oh my gosh! Is it yours? Did you write the script, Wes?"

Wes choked on the idea. "Lord, no!"

"Julia? Did Julia write it?"

"Kani, calm down. Neither of us wrote it. Someone I now did, and I want you to consider it for Ramshackle. Read it tonight, then call me, no matter how late. We've got some ideas if you like the script."

Kani made it through another day, then curled up in bed to read Wes's script. She'd had no idea what to expect. Certainly not this funny, warm, surprisingly emotional story about a young man's search to understand why his mother had abandoned him as a child.

She lay snuggled in bed amidst her usual ten pillows, hugging the script, smiling and crying at the same time. This was it. This poignant tale was the play Ramshackle Theater would end its existence with. She pulled her bedside phone into her lap and dialed the Linnell house.

"Okay, I'm hooked," she said when Wes answered the phone. "Now tell me who wrote it."

He laughed. "Hooked enough to produce it?"

"Definitely. This is our swan song."

"Guaranteed?"

"Do you want it in blood?"

"Blue ink will do."

"So who wrote the damned thing?"

"I can't tell you."

"Wesley." Her voice was a low growl.

"But I can tell you this. This is his first play, he's broke, and he doesn't live in San Francisco so he'd need a place to live during rehearsals."

"He can stay with Bryan and me."

Wes chuckled, a little nastily, Kani thought.

"Robert Vandemere has agreed to direct it."

Kani gasped, choked and sputtered. "Robert Vandemere! *The* Robert Vandemere?"

"Yep."

"Oh my gosh. Why?"

"As a favor to me. And because he liked the script."

"Oh my gosh."

"You don't even have to pay him."

"Oh my gosh."

"*And* we're going to get you citywide coverage in all the media."

"Oh my gosh."

"Your vocabulary has become staggeringly limited, Kani."

There was a full five-second pause. "I hardly know what to say. We're going to go out with a bang instead of a whimper. Thank you, Wes. Thank you so very much."

"I'll get back to you within a few days about the details."

"When do I get to know who the playwright is?"

"When I've talked it over with him. He doesn't know about any of this yet."

"Is there some reason you think he'd object to having his play produced? Isn't that the goal of writing one?"

"For most people, perhaps. I'll call you, Kani."

Kani repeated her thanks, then cradled the phone. There wasn't even a part for her in—what was the title?—oh, yes, *Journeys*. She wouldn't close the theater in front of the footlights; instead, she would hang lights and build the set and sew costumes. She would prompt lines, sell tickets, soothe egos . . . baby-sit a new playwright.

Oh, boy. She hadn't considered that. Talk about soothing egos. Having the playwright there during rehearsals could be immensely valuable; however, a new playwright could also be difficult to handle. But she had an ace in the hole—Robert Vandemere. He would handle the playwright's ego. Kani would handle the business only.

Ahhh, this was going to be perfect. No complications at all.

Seven

———

"Iain MacKenzie!" Kani shrieked. "*That's* the mysterious playwright? The one who will be living here during rehearsals? Tell me this is not the same Iain MacKenzie I met in Mazatlán."

"Kani," Julia began calmly.

"*You* sent us to Mexico, didn't you? You knew we'd meet. I can't believe this of you, Julia. I really can't. You're my *friend.*"

"It was done with the best of intentions. You've been so sad lately, and—"

"Oh, right. And a week of hot sex should cure anyone of *sadness*. Doctors should prescribe it. Insurance companies should pay for it." Kani paced her kitchen, occasionally glaring at Julia and Wes. "It's true I was 'sad,' Julia, but I wasn't in pain. Don't you know what you're doing to me? Do you think the things that attracted me to him before have somehow vanished? He's going to look the same and talk the same. His damned gorgeous hair will still curl down his neck to tease me!" She lifted her arms, then dropped them abruptly, a gesture of complete exasperation. "He's going to smell the same!"

Wes tightened his lips against a smile, not daring a look at Julia. If Kani could still remember Iain's scent, she really was hooked.

"So what did Iain think about this...situation?" she asked.

"He balked. He stonewalled. He argued," Wes said. "Then he realized what an incredible opportunity it is. He agreed—provided we tell you first and let you change your mind if you want."

"He did?" That gave her pause. "Fine. Call him back. Tell him no."

Wes cut off Julia's argument. "Kani, your dream is to close Ramshackle with brilliance. You've been given that opportunity. You can't tell me you don't want this."

"I do want this. I just don't want Iain here. We've never had a playwright involved in a production before. What difference could it make?"

"Maybe because Iain needs this. And I think you realize that. Things have happened in his life lately that have pushed him beyond what most people usually have to endure. He needs a creative outlet. You need a good play."

"I know he lost his job. What else?"

Wes shook his head. "It's not for me to say."

Kani crossed her arms over her chest and let her head droop, feeling sympathy for Iain but determined not to let it influence her unduly. "All right. But he has to stay with you and Julia."

"Coward," Julia said. "I never would have thought it of you. You've always been so adventurous. It's one of the things I've admired about you."

"Impulsive," Kani corrected. "There's a difference. Well, this time I'm thinking with my head first."

"Won't your brother be home soon?"

"Day after tomorrow."

"So Bryan can chaperon. I can't quite picture Iain living in a house with a seven-month-old baby, can you?"

Kani threw her hands into the air again. "I give up! He can stay here. But I'm locking my bedroom door!" *And my heart.*

"Damn."

Iain read the muttered oath on Kani's lips as he walked toward her from across the bar, noting her gaze was focused as intently on him as his was on her.

"Hello, Kani."

"Iain. What can I get you?"

Her professional demeanor momentarily confused him. "Beer."

"Light? Dark? Draft? Imported?"

"Whatever."

He watched her fingers flex around the tall glass as she filled it, and saw the tension radiate from her body, a sleek body that brought back memories of sun and sand and unmatched pleasure.

"How was the drive north?" Tight with stress, her voice was pitched an octave higher, and she looked torn between wishing she'd never seen him again and wanting to throw herself across the bar and into his arms. Her obvious ambivalence made him realize how very fragile her emotions were—and how very carefully he needed to treat her.

"The drive wasn't bad," he said.

She plunked the glass down and named the price, which he paid promptly. She ignored the tip he left; he shoved it into his shirt pocket.

"Why are you here?" she asked pointedly, scooping up a cloth and buffing the bar top. "Wes must have told you where you could find the key."

"He told me. But given the circumstances, I don't know what to believe from him. I wanted to make sure this was really all right with you."

She buffed faster. "I agreed to it."

He laid a hand on hers, stopping her movement, then grimaced as her eyes closed and her lips pressed tightly together.

"Don't touch me," she said, low and feral. "We're doing each other a favor. *That's all.*"

"Need help, chickadee?" Jake moved protectively to her side, an empty wine goblet held weaponlike in his bony fist.

"No. Thanks. He was just leaving."

Something about the man's appearance struck Iain as funny. He looked like a bantam with his feathers ruffled, he decided. Better to make friends than enemies with the keeper of this roost. He stuck out his hand. "Iain MacKenzie. Kani and I met in Mexico."

Jake looked at the proffered hand, then back into Iain's face, purposely ignoring the friendly gesture.

So, you know about me, do you? Iain thought. Strange. He hadn't said a word to anyone about Kani, had only hinted at something to Wes during a phone call his first night home from the trip. Kani had told not only Julia and Wes, but also her co-worker. He lifted his beer again and took a long swallow, feeling like a teenager being inspected by a parent.

After fixing Iain with a cautionary stare, Jake retreated to fix a drink order. Kani took several steps back, then turned from him, as well.

He nursed the beer as he watched Kani work the final hour of her shift. She knew a lot of the customers both by name and by drink, which she mixed with skill, dexterity and a flair for the dramatic. She patted a hand or two, offered a sympathetic ear, slapped a congratulatory high five—and just plain sparkled. Her braid remained neat and lustrous even after eight hours of constant movement; the snazzy red bow tie she wore matched her lipstick, and the satiny cummerbund accentuated her small waist and tempting breasts. He could picture her smooth, tight buttocks, could see her long, silky legs stretched out on a lounge chair, could feel them wrapped around him while they made love....

These next few months were going to be damned difficult, if not impossible, to survive with his sanity intact. If she could just stay mad at him, keep her resentment on the surface, then maybe he could get through it. But to live with her and not touch her, after all they'd shared? Whose idea of a sick joke was this?

Wes and Julia's. He still couldn't believe they'd set him and Kani up like that, paid for their trips just so they would meet. But then to dangle a carrot in front of them, his play, which meant so much to him and could mean a lot to her...

He was worried about finances, though. As gratifying as it was to have his play produced, he wouldn't get much income from it, and he still had to find the money for a house payment, car insurance, gas, food and other basics. He needed a temporary job, fast.

"I'll be right back, then we can go," Kani said as she swept past him.

Jake waited until she'd disappeared before wandering Iain's way. The glass in his hand shone, but he continued to polish it with a fine white cloth. He looked at Iain from beneath lowered brows, his gaze intense and unwavering. "She's a good girl, and that's a fact. You harm her *in any way* and you'll wish yourself dead. You got that?"

"I care about her, too," Iain replied simply.

"I'll be keepin' my eye on you."

Iain had had enough. He jolted upright, leaned tense hands against the edge of the bar, and bent toward his self-appointed judge. "Why the hell doesn't anyone think I could get hurt, too? If I hurt her, I hurt myself. And I'm no masochist."

"What's going on?" Kani asked of the two obviously territorial males having a shoot-out with their eyes. She glanced from one to the other and saw them each relax, inch by inch, without giving an inch.

"We were gettin' acquainted," Jake said, a warning in his voice.

Out of respect for Kani's obvious friendship with the old codger, Iain refrained from snorting his disbelief. Jake considered the issuing of threats as getting acquainted, did he? Iain turned his attention on Kani, who stood with a worried expression marring her beautiful face. "I'll walk you to your car, then follow you."

"I took the bus. I'd appreciate a ride home."

"No problem. Jake, it was nice meeting you." This time when he extended his hand, Jake took it reluctantly, but firmly. "See you."

"That's a fact," Jake replied.

Iain and Kani walked in silence and, aside from Kani making a brief statement about how foolish he'd been to leave his car full of his belongings where anyone could break into it, they drove in near silence, with only directions being asked for and given succinctly. Kani climbed out of the car and opened the garage door. She tossed him a spare electric opener as he got out of the car, then quickly turned away. She climbed the stairs, opened the door, then returned to help him carry in his things.

Gypsy uncurled from her basket bed, arched in a huge stretch, and yawned, blinking at them as they made several silent trips in and out of the house. Kani put Iain in the only downstairs bedroom, as far away from hers as she could get him.

After putting away his clothes, he left his computer to be hooked up later and exited the room. It was a great old house, Victorian in style but contemporary in furnishings. Splashy art hung on the walls; brilliant Oriental rugs lay on glossy hardwood floors; furniture that was both sleek and comfortable looking filled the living and dining rooms. Interesting objets d'art held places of prominence on tables and pedestals. While none of it seemed much like Kani to him, he admired the look of the house.

He could hear Kani moving around upstairs, wondered how long she would avoid him, and planted himself in a chair to wait her out. The moment he sat down, a fluffy ball of gray fur climbed his leg, balanced precariously on his thigh, and stared at him.

"So I have to pass your test, too, do I? Another defender of her virtue, hmm?" He scratched the kitten's ears as he whispered, "I have news for you. It's too late."

Gypsy tossed her head as if indignant, leapt off his lap, then zoomed up the stairs and meowed until Kani let her into the bedroom.

He smelled her perfume first, the scent drifting downstairs and sending him reeling back to Mazatlán. His passion for her hadn't surprised him—he'd known from the moment he saw her that physically they would be in sync. Her exuberance for life, her love of people, her joy in simple moments, had been an unexpected pleasure.

What had surprised him most, though, was the peace he'd felt with her. Peace. What a rare commodity, especially in *his* life. But he had found peace with her as they'd read their books side by side, as they'd eaten leisurely meals, and especially, most especially, after they'd made love.

He'd written about such peacefulness, seen it portrayed in movies, but he hadn't really believed it existed. Then, that first morning after they'd made love, he'd discovered the luxurious warmth of peace. And he missed it now as much as he missed the passion.

Her legs came into view at the top of the stairs. High heels, then a good length of tanned legs, which disappeared into the hem of a minidress—the same dress she'd worn when they'd gone to Señor Frog's, the same damn dress he'd peeled off her with unhurried care. What was she up to? he wondered, as she made her way slowly down the stairs, revealing herself by inches. Shoes, endless legs, snug-fitting dress, bare arms, too much uncovered skin, her hair down... and flowing... and curling... and enticing.

He didn't move, couldn't move. He was instantly, painfully, fiercely aroused, even as he wondered what her game was.

Her chin notched upward. "I have a date," she announced, daring him to comment.

Remember, old man, you want to keep her angry. "Have fun."

"I intend to." She handed him a sheet of paper. "We have an appointment with Robert Vandemere tomorrow night at eight at the theater. Here's his phone number and address, as well as other pertinent numbers. Auditions will be held Sunday and Monday at the theater. You're welcome to whatever food you find in the kitchen.'' She tossed him a key ring. ''House, garage, theater. I usually go to the gym at seven-thirty in the morning, then straight to work. So I probably won't see you until after work tomorrow.''

''I'll survive,'' he said, and watched her body stiffen. Gypsy jumped onto his lap and instantly curled into a tight ball, tucking her head beneath a paw. Iain stroked the soft fur with gentle fingers.

Traitor, Kani thought, jealous of Gypsy's position. *What I'd give to take your place!* ''Good night, then,'' she said firmly, tucking her clutch purse under her arm. When he just stared at her, she leaned down to pet Gypsy, bumping fingers with his, then bent farther to kiss the top of her head. '''Night, baby.''

Iain watched her head bow over his lap, felt the weight of her hair fall against his legs, breathed in her scent, and silently begged her to kiss him, too. She lifted her head slowly, her mouth mere inches from his, her lightly painted lips parted and inviting, the tip of her tongue touching the roof of her mouth.

He said nothing. She left in silence.

He listened to a car start below him in the garage, then he sat for at least ten minutes before he set Gypsy on the floor and headed to the kitchen. ''Whatever food you find'' didn't amount to much—canned soup, fresh fruit, bread. He could call Wes and go visit him and Julia...and the baby. He wasn't too sure about the baby, never having spent any time around one. Didn't they cry a lot? And spit up formula? Maybe another time, he decided. He remembered the Chinese take-out place they'd passed as they'd driven home earlier, perhaps a mile away.

''If you were a dog, I'd take you for a walk,'' he told the kitten. Restless and in need of physical exertion to shatter the tension radiating through his body, he made a quick detour to his bedroom to grab a city map, then headed out.

Although he had visited San Francisco before, he hadn't spent enough time there to know his way around well, but he'd always been amazed by the contrasts between this city and Southern California. As he walked he noted the differences. There were hills in Southern California, but they were scattered, not an everyplace occurrence. Although it was crowded down south, the homes didn't butt up against each other as they did here. And it was cool here, even in July, unlike the usually mild, sometimes hot weather of his home. San Francisco seemed almost a foreign country.

At the restaurant he studied the menu, bought the least expensive but most healthful items, learned the owners' names, then headed back toward the house. A block away from the restaurant, he glanced down a side street and noticed a sign: Ramshackle Theater.

Drawn, he headed that way. The building was a small converted warehouse painted robin's egg blue and decorated with a series of characters in theatrical costumes from many different eras—from three Shakespearean witches to a Webber Phantom. Unless he missed his guess, Julia Linnell had done the artwork.

He inserted one of the keys in the door and was rewarded—it was the right one. However, he discovered the door was unlocked. Silently he moved into the building, past the ticket counter, the drinking fountain that hummed as it cooled the water and the rest rooms with their Romeo-and-Juliet-painted doors. He followed sounds of grumbling and of wood being tossed until he was drawn into the theater itself, with its two hundred seats, curtainless stage and overhead maze of lights and catwalks. On he continued, following the voice and the *thwack* of wood hitting wood, and climbing stairs to reach the stage, striding across the expanse to the left wing and into the scene shop.

He recognized that derriere. Kani, wearing snug blue jeans and T-shirt, with her hair pulled into a ponytail, was rearranging two-by-fours by height against a wall. He kept walking until he could pluck a fifteen-foot-long plank from her and heave it aside.

"What the—? Iain!" Kani shrank into herself. *Caught.*
Caught in a big fat lie about having a date. Caught by the
man she wanted most to mislead.

He leaned into her, his face full of fury. "Don't you ever,
ever do that again. God, what a stupid thing to do."

Eight

Kani cringed at the fierceness of his voice, at the intensity of his expression.

"Do you know, do you have any idea, how many maniacs are out there?" he all but screamed at her. "You're in here all by yourself with the damned door unlocked! Damn you and your trust in your fellow human beings. Don't you know you can't trust anyone?"

Embarrassed both at being caught in her lie and at having left the door unlocked, she reacted not with gratitude that he was looking out for her but with anger. "I guess I've learned that the hard way."

He drew in a deep breath. "There's a difference between big-bad-wolf types like me and those who intend you physical harm."

Kani relented. "I usually do lock the door. But tonight I was...preoccupied." She turned to the woodpile and began sorting again.

He waited until his pulse stopped thrumming in his head and his fists uncurled before he dared speak again. Even then he had to blow out a deep, calming breath first. "Ar you hungry? It's probably cold by now, but I've got enoug dinner here to share."

Her stomach growled on cue. She sighed. "We've got microwave." She tugged off her gloves and tucked them int her back pocket, then led the way to the makeshift kitche normally used to prepare prop food. *So when is he going t say something snide about my not being on a date?* sh wondered dismally. Surely he wouldn't pass up a chance t taunt her.

But by the time she'd reheated the food, dug out som paper plates and plastic forks, and poured them some soda he hadn't mentioned it at all, had only asked question about the theater itself.

She couldn't take it a minute longer. "Why haven't yo given me a bad time about lying to you?"

He chewed thoughtfully, staring at her, noting the bellig erent posture and the embarrassed flush on her face. H kept his voice casual. "Your hackles are up enough al ready. I don't expect anything I say would help. But if i means anything, I understand why you did it, and we don' need to talk about it."

His sensitivity was her undoing. Tears sparkled in her eye as she focused on her food, not looking up to meet the in tense gaze she felt directed on her. "Thanks," she choke out.

"I know I hurt you, Kani, but we're not enemies."

He stayed to help her organize the scene shop, talking lit tle, taking care not to touch. It was after eleven when the got home. Iain was exhausted; he'd left Hollywood at seve that morning, and the grueling, emotionally charged da had caught up with him.

Pushing open the front door for Kani, he let her pass i front of him, breathed her fragrance, and briefly closed hi eyes. God, he wished they were sharing a bed. He needer her, needed her innocence, needed her loving. Needed th peace.

"Bryan!"

Iain watched Kani fly across the room and into the arms of an Arnold Schwarzenegger look-alike only to be spun around in a far-too-familiar embrace. Jealousy clobbered him over the head. He'd never known jealousy before—not one iota of it. Women came and went, and it hadn't mattered what they did or who they saw, even when their relationship had been at the most heated stage.

But at this moment he was seeing red.

Through the haze, he noted the familiar way the man stroked Kani's ponytail.

"Where's my car?" Mr. America asked.

"In the garage, safe and sound."

"Would have been nice to have it my first night home."

"Since when? You usually just want to go straight to bed."

The haze turned crimson.

"I slept the whole flight just so I wouldn't need to go to bed instantly. Well, not to sleep, anyway."

The haze was now incarnadine.

"So why didn't you invite Caroline here?"

He tapped a finger on her nose. "Believe it or not, sometimes a man wants more than a quiet evening behind closed doors."

That the man lived here was obvious, Iain thought, but his red haze was dissipating at their continued conversation. Had they been lovers? Apparently they no longer were.

"Iain," Kani was repeating, drawing him out of his stupor, "this is my brother, Bryan Warner. Bryan, Iain MacKenzie. He's staying with us for a while."

Brother! Of course. If he hadn't reacted so irrationally, he would have seen the resemblance, a resemblance that ended with their eyes. Where Kani's were open and guileless, Bryan's seemed to use some inner force to seek answers to unasked questions. Iain held his ground, shaking the extended hand and returning the searching gaze with shuttered eyes. No one had been allowed access to his soul, ever.

Bryan smiled slightly. In approval? Iain wondered. In recognition of a kindred spirit? Whatever—something clicked, and with it came a remarkable trust, although he neither understood nor wanted it.

"What does 'staying with us for a while' mean?" Bryan asked.

"We're going to produce a play Iain wrote. Robert Vandemere is going to direct."

Bryan whistled. "Nice going, sis. He's big time."

"Well, it wasn't my doing. Wes and Julia arranged it."

"I should have guessed. Where are you from, Iain?"

"Hollywood." The moment they were all seated in the living room, Gypsy jumped onto Iain's lap.

"Have you had other plays produced?"

"No. Wes is a friend of mine. He read it, liked it, and talked Kani into staging it."

"He didn't have to talk me into it, Iain. I loved it, too. It's a powerful story of love and pain and growth." She cocked her head at him. "Is it autobiographical? I understand that many first plays are—sort of a cathartic exercise."

"I'm there in bits and pieces." He always gave this stock answer to those who asked. That the play was almost completely autobiographical was no one's business but his. *Only the names have been changed to protect the innocent.* "It's impossible for a writer to exclude the self completely."

"Was it a long project?" Bryan asked.

"Eight years, off and on. So, have you been away on business or pleasure?"

Bryan shrugged. "A combination of both. I dabble in a few things. Takes me all over the world. All told, I'm gone half the year. Kani keeps the home fires burning and the car maintained. Homecoming is an adventure since I never know how many strays she's taken in while I've been gone."

"Not strays, just people in need of temporary housing." She turned to Iain. "I think we should share, don't you? And I like having company."

Bryan looked at his watch before he stood. "Caroline is waiting so I'll say good-night. Iain, I can get you a guest membership at my gym while you're here. Interested?"

"Depends on the cost. I'm a little short on funds at the moment." Iain forced casualness into the words. It was humiliating to have lost everything as he had.

Bryan shoved his hands into his pockets. "When I said 'my gym,' I meant it literally. I'm part owner. No charge for a friend. Or a scrawny sister," he added with a grin.

"Scrawny," Iain repeated without thinking. "One of the first things I noticed about her was her...muscles...." His voice faded as he realized what he'd said, and he took a moment to move Gypsy from his lap to the crook of his arm.

Bryan glanced from Iain to Kani. His mouth quirked. "C'mere and give me a hug," he ordered his sister, and she happily let herself be crushed in his embrace. He kept his arm around her as they walked to the front door. Quietly he said, "He's a far cry from your usual stray. Are you okay?"

She nodded against his chest.

"Why don't I believe that?" He squeezed her arm and released her. "Save some time for me, okay? I want to hear all about your trip to Mexico. And what Iain means to you—and why."

Kani opened her mouth to deny everything, but when she caught his sympathetic yet insistent gaze she relented. "Yes, sir." She sniffed his cheek as she kissed it. "Uh-oh. Got the killer cologne on. Guess I'll see you when you finally come up for air."

He grinned and wiggled his eyebrows before he passed through the doorway.

Kani locked the door and turned around, only to find Iain standing behind her. She clasped her hands. "I imagine you're worn-out."

"Yes." *But not too tired to make love to you.*

"Big day tomorrow."

"Have you met Vandemere?"

"No," she said, "although I've heard a lot about him from theater friends. Demanding, but fair. Wondrousl creative—that sort of stuff. I'm sure he'll give your play th treatment it deserves."

"I'm not worried about it." He passed the sleeping kit ten to Kani, taking care not to touch her. "I've rarely en vied anyone or anything, but I envy you and Bryan."

Kani cocked her head. "Why?"

"I don't have a sibling, but if I did, I'd want a relation ship like yours. I can't even imagine it—to be close to on person your entire life, to know you can count on them al ways."

Kani nodded thoughtfully. "There are very few people i this world you can really count on," she agreed. "Throug thick and thin. In sickness and in health."

To love and to cherish, he thought. "Till death do yo part."

Kani swallowed. How was she supposed to stay mad a him when he showed her his vulnerabilities and treated he so gently? *Damn you, Iain MacKenzie!* "Good night," sh said abruptly before sidestepping by him and jogging up th stairs.

She was almost out of sight when he called her name. Sh turned slowly.

"Do you mind if I tag along with you to the gym tomor row?"

"I guess not. Be ready to leave at seven-fifteen. I wall there."

"Fine."

"Fine."

Iain smiled at her polite and proper demeanor. "Good night, Average," he said, then walked away before she could form a response. *Great job of keeping her angry, old man,* he chastised himself halfheartedly. But how in the world do you keep a gentle soul like Kani angry without being a complete jerk? *And since when has it mattered?*

* * *

At first they didn't say much during their fifteen-minute walk to the gym. Sleep well? Fine. You? Fine.

Liars, both.

Iain had heard muted television sounds from above, then Kani moving around her room several times during the night, because he'd been awake pacing his. Exhausted as he'd been, sleep had tempted but hadn't come for more than an hour at a time. He'd become too accustomed to her, too fast, in Mexico. At home, he'd spent every night tossing and turning, tangling the sheets and waking exhausted.

And now, now being just below her, a twenty-second walk from her bed, her warmth, her passion—well, how much could he endure?

"Will I be your guest today?" he asked about ten minutes into their walk.

"Bryan will have left a message on the answering machine last night for whoever opens up this morning. He's good about things like that, you know, details."

"What sort of things does he 'dabble' in?"

"I have no idea. I've learned not to ask. Don't raise your eyebrows at me, Iain. He's not a criminal. He does security stuff, high-level, top secret. I don't ask questions because he can't give me answers. Sometimes he can't tell me where he is, but he always calls and checks in. He's very thoughtful. And I have a phone number where someone can reach him in an emergency."

"How long have you shared a house?"

"Oh gosh, almost forever. My mom and stepfather moved to Arizona when I was eighteen. Bryan had been living on his own for five years. He bought the house from them and invited me to be his roommate. I had to sell my car, so he insists I use his while he's away, but I seldom do."

"Why don't you have a car?"

"I sold it to help finance Ramshackle when my last two partners left town."

"The theater's been losing money?"

"Yes, somewhat. But what's made it difficult is my having sole responsibility. Four of us started it as equal partners. We each had our own talents and jobs, but one by one the others moved on. It's too much for just me, and I haven't been able to get anyone else interested. At least, interested enough to help with the financial obligations. In a lot of ways, I'm looking forward to it closing. I'll finally have extra money and time."

"Have you really accepted the loss?"

She hesitated in answering.

"Kani?" he prompted.

Her gaze avoided his. "I won't miss the responsibility."

"But?" he pressed.

She drew a deep breath as she voiced her feelings aloud for the first time. "But I feel like such a failure."

"Because you couldn't do the job of *four people?*"

"There's no need for sarcasm, Iain. In my head I know I've been asking the impossible of myself. In my heart...in my heart I have to accept the loss of my family. That's what theater companies become, you know—especially community theaters where no one is paid. We were all in it for the personal satisfaction and the camaraderie. The plays that were successes sustained us through the bombs. We were really tight for a long time. Now everything's changed. It's time to move on."

"To what?"

To a home of my own, with a husband who loves me, and children to cherish. Her dream had reached epic proportions. She was more than hungry for a family of her own; she was starved. But she knew that this man had neither the desire nor the need to share her dream.

"To whatever the future holds," Kani answered him at last.

"Won't you miss it?"

"I expect to keep my hand in it. I'll probably audition and volunteer at other community theaters occasionally. They're always looking for backstage help, and I've gotten pretty

good at swinging a hammer and climbing twenty-foot lad-
ders.''

"No thoughts of going to New York or Hollywood?"

Kani wondered at the tightness in his voice but answered
with a laugh. "I'm not that talented."

"That's not what Julia says."

"You didn't hear sarcasm in her voice? She had to have
been kidding. I'm a mediocre actor and have no singing
ability whatsoever. I can dance, though. That's my forte.
Here we are."

They passed two men and a woman in business attire
carrying sports bags; the woman wore sneakers with her
summer-weight tweed jacket and skirt.

"I like to come this time of day because the early birds are
just finishing up before getting off to work and the night
owls haven't rolled out of bed yet," she told Iain as they
signed in at the front desk. "See, I told you he'd call. Bryan
doesn't forget anything."

Kani grunted a greeting at Julia when Julia joined her an
hour later at the stair-climbing machine.

"How're things going?" Julia asked.

"It's only been a day," Kani replied.

"And you can't take your eyes off each other."

Kani's gaze shifted abruptly from Iain's lanky form to
Julia, who looked entirely too self-satisfied. Kani draped
herself over the handlebars, then burrowed her face into a
towel before patting her chest and arms to absorb the rivu-
lets of sweat. "I know what you're getting at, Julia. But this
mating game isn't gonna work. He doesn't want someone
permanent. I don't want anyone who won't be. This is the
end of the line for me."

"Kani—"

"I mean it. Every man I've been romantically involved
with has hurt me, Iain included. I'm tired of being a play-
thing. And Iain's lack of stability, both in his career and his
finances, indicates he's just not husband material. *And I
want a husband.*"

"But you're in love with him."

"That's debatable." *Liar, liar, pants on fire. Well, that's another problem, isn't it—hot pants?*

"I know you're not as mercenary as you sound, Kani. Why won't you let yourself stay in love with him, be with him?"

Kani slung the towel around the back of her neck and held an end in each hand. Wet tendrils of hair clung to her jaw and neck. She leaned into her friend, forcing her to stop climbing. Her expression held pain and annoyance and frustration. "Because if I let myself be with him again and he left me, *I would never recover.*"

"And if you don't let yourself be with him again, your chance for hearth and home with him are gone like yesterday's garbage."

"I can't, Julia. I just can't." The words were squeezed painfully from her. "This play will start a new career for him. He'll be off to New York just like Nathan and John Q." Kani tried to conjure up images of her two old boyfriends and found only Iain's visage, a fact that infuriated her. "Damn him. Damn you. I'm trying to protect myself. Let me. Please."

Julia raised both hands. "Not another word." She watched Kani relax. "For now."

Kani choked on a laugh, the tension shattered. "I don't know why I put up with you. I really don't."

"Because I'm one of the few who'll give it to you straight. Now tell me what you thought of Carlotta and Daniel's big news yesterday."

At the mention of the soap opera characters, Kani launched into an emotional tirade on the strange turn the characters' relationship had taken. "There's no motivation. Nothing's led up to it."

"Not only that," Julia said, "but they're resurrecting a plot they used years ago. Remember? Only then they used Jackson and Ariel."

"I know! What a dumb thing to do when there are endless story ideas out there." Kani had become addicted to the daytime serial "A Time to Love" five years earlier when she'd had her appendix out. Her hospital roommate, a longtime fan, had shared each character's biography. That was all Kani needed. She'd been hooked ever since, so much so that she taped the show every day and watched it every night right before bed. The show had the same effect as a tranquilizer, letting her unwind with someone else's problems. And, oh, how she loved the weddings!

"What's a dumb thing to to?" Iain asked as he came up beside them. He'd been watching Kani and Julia talk, had noted the changing expressions on their faces and the way Kani jerked the chrome weights she'd just picked up rather than curling and methodically lifting them.

"Don't mind us," Julia said, laughing. "We get a little emotional about our soap opera."

"Which one is that?"

"'A Time to Love.'"

His show! Iain held his breath, then released it gradually as he caught Kani's arm, slowing her jerky movements. "Are you in a race? So tell me what was dumb."

"Like you'd really be interested."

"Actually I am. I have a friend in the cast, but I've missed seeing it for about six weeks." *Couldn't face seeing it.*

Kani eyed him skeptically. "You actually watch 'A Time to Love'?"

"I've followed it for about six years."

Her expression turned downright suspicious. "Who's your friend in the cast?"

"Gayle Alexander. She plays Carlotta."

Jealousy smacked Kani in the face. Gayle Alexander was about the sexiest woman on television. *What kind of friend? How close a friend?* Kani wanted to ask. Her weights picked up speed again.

"Then you'll understand when we tell you what they did to Carlotta and Daniel in yesterday's show," she said to Iain while trying to tamp down her jealousy.

Iain plucked the once again fast-moving weights from her hands. "You're doing more harm than good, don't you think? I've never seen anyone exercise like you do. Now tell me what they did to Carlotta."

Kani and Julia denounced the latest story shift, stepping on each other's sentences, threatening to stop watching the show, practically insisting he agree that what the writers had done was *criminal*.

Silently Iain agreed. Certainly the story shift hadn't been in the plans when he'd been fired, and most ideas were plotted months in advance. What had happened that they needed to twist the plot so dramatically and suddenly? Should he call Gayle? Or was he better off just letting it go? Despite the ribbing he'd endured from his friends while he was writing for the show, he'd been proud of what he'd done and pleased when someone wrote to say thanks, that they'd learned to face a problem of their own because of how they'd handled it on the show. Even the parties that fans had while they watched the big weddings were fun to hear about—it meant the writers had done a good job of making the characters seem real. What more could a writer ask?

"Personally, I think you should call your friend," Kani interrupted his musings to say, "and tell her if they let this plot continue, I'll... I'll fast-forward through all of their scenes!"

Iain laughed at her threat. Such passion, such fire in her gold-dusted eyes. "I'm sure finding out she'd be just a blur on your television set would be enough to send her to the producer."

"So do it. Oh my gosh, I'm gonna be late for work. I'll meet you at the theater by eight, Iain, if I don't see you at home first."

Julia followed more slowly but first turned to Iain, who had watched Kani run off. "She's a bit impulsive. But that doesn't mean she's flighty. There's more commitment in that woman than in two or three people combined. And she'll tolerate all kinds of mistakes from everyone else but cut herself no slack at all. If there's blame to be taken for something, she'll take it—even if she was a hundred miles from the scene of the crime."

"She doesn't cut me any slack, either."

Julia smiled as she sauntered off. "She doesn't, does she?"

Iain frowned. What the hell was that supposed to mean?

"He's rather mesmerizing, isn't he?" Kani asked of Iain as they walked home from their meeting with Robert Vandemere.

"I'd call him intimidating."

"Well, he certainly knows what he wants. Does his interpretation of the play bother you? He seemed to be making statements, not asking questions."

Iain shrugged. "I think we'll discuss it more when the actors are chosen and we begin serious characterization. For now, his vision's all right with me."

Kani looked askance at him. "You're about the most flexible playwright I've ever come across. You don't seem to care if he changes words, or sequence, or anything."

"He gave good reasons and I agreed with him. Even though I've been working on it for eight years, it's still a work-in-progress, Kani. I never intended for it to be produced at all. I guess that's why I'm more open about it than others might be."

"You never intended—" she repeated in amazement. "Seriously?"

"It was just an idea that came to me, and I worked on it whenever the mood struck. It was nothing critical to me."

"You mean you don't have a stack of scripts at home waiting to be staged on the heels of this success?"

"Not one," he replied cheerfully. "Not even an idea for one."

"What kind of a playwright are you?"

"A one-play wonder? Is that so bad? Why not write one really good play rather than ten mediocre ones?"

"Because the quality of this play proves you wouldn't write mediocre ones."

His mouth quirked at the corner. "I appreciate the faith. We'll see."

"Were you surprised Robert wants you to have equal say in casting?"

Iain laughed. "I think he'll give the *illusion* of granting me equal say. He'll do the choosing. Tell me, how much would a director of his caliber normally receive for directing a play?"

"I have no idea. Why?"

"I can't figure out why he's doing it. The play's not *that* good."

"The play *is* that good, Iain. But you know Wes. He's got so many contacts and so many favors he can call in, I wouldn't be surprised if Robert owed him one."

They had reached the house. Iain paused with his hand on the knob. "We've had two civilized conversations. Think it can continue?"

"Of course. Why wouldn't it?"

Why not, indeed, Iain thought. *Just because my heart starts dancing a jig every time I'm with you. Just because my arms ache to hold you. Just because I want to wake up with you in my arms.* Just because he was frustrated with longing for this multidimensional, fascinating woman who felt as strongly about fictional soap opera characters as she did about offering shelter to someone in need.

He spoke matter-of-factly. "I was hoping you wouldn't mind if I watch 'A Time to Love' with you tonight. I'd like to see the program once before I call Gayle."

Kani swallowed. She and Bryan both owned VCRs, but they were connected to their bedroom televisions. Have Iain in her bedroom? No way.

They moved into the kitchen to fix a snack. "How about this, Iain? I'll set up the tape again after I'm done, then you can watch it tomorrow while I'm at work."

Iain perused the meager contents of the refrigerator as she spoke. He turned his head and stared at her with such intensity that she squirmed.

She forced her body to be still. "You make it seem so casual, Iain, and it's anything but. I'm making every effort to have a friendly relationship with you so that we can work together for the success of the play. But don't ask me for more than that."

He shut the refrigerator door and leaned a shoulder against it. "If I want to talk to Gayle, I have to call her by 5:00 a.m., before she heads for the soundstage."

"So watch it tomorrow and call her the next day."

"Coward." His voice was softly accusing.

Kani was sick of people accusing her of cowardice when she was only interested in self-preservation, which was a different issue altogether. She threw her hands into the air. "All right. All *right*. You can watch it tonight with me."

She turned abruptly and left the room, leaving him to do what? Follow like a puppy? Iain stood for several seconds debating how to approach her—humbly, boldly, silently, instantly? She was damned hard to figure out.

Kani was grumbling to Gypsy, who sat in the middle of her bed cocking her head as if every word Kani uttered was critical. Iain stopped in the open doorway, a bowl in each hand, waiting to be invited in.

"Can't even curl up in bed to watch," he heard her say belligerently. "Can't put my nightgown on. Can't relax."

He cleared his throat.

Kani spun toward the door, shocked he was there. She hadn't heard him climb the stairs, hadn't heard him approach the room. Her mouth watered at the bowls of vanilla ice cream topped with fresh peach slices he'd fixed. Her gaze switched from the bowls to his face.

He glanced at the enormous mound of pillows piled against the headboard and each other as if they were in some concubine's boudoir, then briefly noted the eclectic furnishings. Not quite frilly, not quite old-fashioned, not quite messy—this was the one room distinctly hers. It made sense to him now why the rest of the house hadn't seemed like Kani. The rest was Bryan's. The souvenirs were from his trips, the decor suited to his tastes.

He liked Kani's bedroom very much.

"You can get into your pj's and into bed as far as I'm concerned."

"What a truly selfless and generous gesture, Iain." Her words dripped sarcasm.

He laughed. "Ice cream's melting."

As he zigzagged the bowl teasingly under her nose, she could smell the touch of cinnamon he'd sprinkled over the fruit. She grabbed the bowl mid-zig, plopped cross-legged onto one side of the bed, and snatched up the remote control. "A gourmet chef, too? What a multitalented man you are."

"This is hardly gourmet." He stood, unsure where she expected him to sit; a quick reconnaissance had revealed no chair. "Where do you want me?"

She patted the bed beside her, then pressed Play on the remote control.

Iain's brows lifted in surprise, but he kicked off his shoes, lowered himself onto the handmade quilt, and leaned back into the mound of pillows. He shifted his shoulders to get comfortable, crossed his ankles, then was joined by Gypsy, who promptly stretched out along the valley his thighs made, her head pillowed on his knees.

He tried not to—oh, how he tried not to—but he couldn't help watching Kani eat, spoonful after spoonful. First she'd pull most of the ice cream into her mouth, then she'd lick the utensil clean, her tongue stroking the smooth silver bowl of the spoon with unconscious sensuality. Intent on the television program, she never turned her head or even relaxed into the pillows. She leaned toward the TV set in total absorption, occasionally making a comment or laughing. She was fascinating to watch. And damned arousing.

Paying scant attention to the program, Iain found himself fantasizing stripping off the T-shirt and sweatpants she'd replaced her skirt and blouse with. He couldn't see a bra line, but the skimpy scraps of silk and lace she'd worn in Mexico wouldn't necessarily be visible through the fabric. Then she took his empty bowl, stacked it with hers and leaned away from him to place them on the floor.

No bra. What cruel game was she playing?

Nine

Arousal came hard and fast; so did Iain's breathing.

Gypsy quivered, lost in a kitten dream, and Kani reached over automatically to soothe her. "Having a bad dream, baby? It's all right." She stroked the kitten repeatedly, not watching her, her hand following a smooth line down Gypsy's back and along her long tail.

Accidentally, unconsciously, she brushed the rigid bulge in Iain's lap. Startled, she lifted her hand. Iain's hand came down hard on hers, pressing hers over his arousal, molding her fingers around him. He sucked in a deep breath and closed his eyes, loving the agony.

She had tried to forget how he felt, hot steel and velvet promising the fulfillment of dreams and desires. She'd tried to forget the silky softness of his lips as he'd aroused her with explosive ardor. And she'd tried, tried very hard, to forget the enticing scent of him. Useless effort, all of it.

The vividness of her memories refused to be muted by time or distance or anger. And this was no memory. He was beside her, wanting her as she wanted him. But she was afraid of the pain that would inevitably come.

The hand covering hers encouraged her to do more than just blanket him, and she rotated and pressed her palm against him, loving the way he arched into her hand. His free hand scooped under her T-shirt and cupped a breast, thumbing the taut nipple and savoring its twin briefly before shoving the fabric up so he could see her.

"Kani," he breathed shakily. Vivid tan line; firm, creamy-skinned breasts; dusky crests tightened into hard buds. He groaned at the sight even as he pushed her hand off his aroused body before her ministrations sent him out of control. He slid his hand into her sweatpants.

No underwear, either.

Their gazes locked as he stroked her with sensitive fingertips, and she instantly began to writhe, catching her breath as the sensations built furiously fast. He knew exactly how to touch, how to stroke, how to probe, until she threw her head back and pressed forward, rotating and arching, instantly peaking.

"Come inside me," she whispered, shoving her pants down over her hips, wanting to feel his power from within.

He helped her slide the garment off. Desire deepened his voice. "Do you have any protection?"

"I'm on the Pill, Iain. You know that." She reached for his jeans and struggled to unbutton them.

"And I told you I don't take chances. I'll be right back."

She grabbed his wrist. "No."

"No?" He shook off the intensity of his arousal. "Yes, Kani."

It was the hardest thing she'd ever done, denying him. "I told you I'm on the Pill. I won't get pregnant."

"Nothing is one hundred percent effective."

"Is it that, or is it that you don't believe I'm on the Pill? Take a chance with me." *Show me you trust me, Iain. I need that from you, if nothing else.*

"You didn't fight it in Mexico." Desire was fading fast at their serious discussion. He watched her tug her sweatpants up over her hips. "I've never had sex without a condom."

"Never?"

"Never. I don't want children. I never have." *Love dies— and children pay for it.*

Strike two. No trust. No children, Kani thought. She didn't need a strike three; two were enough for her. Painful disappointment shot through her.

"I'm sorry for you, Iain. Incredibly sorry. You have no idea what you're missing." *Because no woman could ever love you more than I do, and no woman would be more proud to give you children than I.* She rolled away, turning her back on him, not moving until she heard his bedroom door close downstairs.

Tears refused to come from the dry well of her soul. One of the late-night talk shows came on and she left the television going just for the noise. An hour later, Bryan knocked softly on her door. She pretended to be asleep as he tiptoed in and turned off the TV, then crouched beside her as she lay fully dressed on the quilt.

"You're not asleep," he said gently, reaching out to stroke her hair. He turned briefly, sweeping the room in one glance. "Iain's been here."

"We watched TV for a little while." She kept her eyes closed.

"More than that."

"Don't interfere, Bryan."

He hesitated at the fierceness in her voice. "Want to talk?"

"No." Her voice cracked on a sob, then she threw her arms around him. "What's wrong with me? Just tell me what's wrong with me."

Iain sat at the kitchen table, his hands wrapped around a mug of coffee. When he occasionally lifted it and swallowed, it was out of habit, not for the enjoyment of the rich flavor or the jolt of caffeine.

Another sleepless night. How long until the ravages of sleep deprivation overtook him? God, what a fool! What a damned fool. *You were supposed to keep her angry, old man. Now look what you've done.* Well, he'd gotten what he wanted, and then some—Kani at arm's length, Kani avoiding him, Kani probably hating him.

How had he let his desires take over as they had last night? He'd never, *ever,* lost control like that. How could he possibly make it up to her? How could he get her to be his friend again? Hell, he'd be lucky to be allowed to continue living here.

"You look like you wish that was whiskey," Bryan said, joining Iain at the table, mug in hand.

Iain lifted his head slowly. The last thing he needed this morning was another "brotherly" chat. He'd already endured one from bartender Jake, the father surrogate; even Gypsy had cautioned him with her big yellow eyes.

"Not talkative in the morning?" Bryan continued. "Fine. I'll talk. You listen."

Iain wiped a weary hand down his face, leaned an elbow on the table and pressed a fist to his mouth. His belligerent gaze met Bryan's surprisingly nonjudgmental one.

"Only a blind man would fail to notice how close my sister and I are. We don't really spend much time together when you add it up, but the bond holds. I've watched her make some big mistakes, watched her heart break, watched her heal, all the while not losing her joy for life. She's amazingly resilient. This time I'm afraid for her.

"When her first serious relationship ended—I think she was twenty-two or twenty-three—she bounced back fast. She realized quickly that Nathan hadn't been as committed as she was. She dated a lot after that but nothing serious. After a few years, she was bowled over by an actor with an ego the size of the Golden Gate Bridge. I knew, I was certain, that he was going to hurt her, and I couldn't do anything to stop it. When John Q took off without even telling her—"

Iain couldn't help it. He started to laugh. "John Q? John *Q?* What the hell kind of name is that?"

Bryan smiled. "An egotistical one."

"That's for sure," Iain said lightly, trying to picture Kani whispering *I love you, John Q.* The thought sobered him. Had she said that? Had she told that egotistical bastard she loved him?

"I take it the image bothers you a little," Bryan said, seeing into Iain's mind with uncanny accuracy.

Iain straightened in the chair, somber and reflective. "To be honest, I don't know how I feel about anything right now."

"So I gathered. But you must know what a danger you represent to Kani."

"I have nothing to offer her, Bryan. Only myself."

"She'd be happy with that."

"Would you? As a man, would you let yourself fall for a woman who deserves the sun and the moon and the stars, if all you could give her was a look through a telescope? She deserves more than me."

"And if you *could* give her the tangibles you speak of?"

Iain stood abruptly and moved to lean his hands against the sink, staring outside at the postage-stamp-size backyard. "I'm still not the man for her. She wants more than I can give her."

"Nothing that money can buy." A calculated pause preceded his next words. "I ran a check on you yesterday."

Iain's mouth quirked into a lopsided grin. "Why doesn't that surprise me? Find anything interesting?"

"I imagine you know what I found. Maybe I can help, Iain. I have a lot of contacts."

"There's not much to tell. The person I trusted the most and the longest embezzled almost every cent I had. So far no one's traced him."

Their conversation lasted long enough for Iain to lose his defensive edge and get comfortable as he shared the details of his financial situation with Bryan. Again he felt a stab of

envy at the closeness of the siblings, of the love and protec-
tiveness they shared.

No one had ever stood up for him, or looked out for him.

He balanced on the back two legs of the kitchen chair and
rocked slowly, wondering what it would have been like having a brother or sister to share a history with. He shook the
idea from his head—he would never even have an in-law.
"Kani says you do high-level security work, and I can only
guess what that means, especially since you're out of the
country a lot. I'd appreciate whatever you could come up
with."

Bryan slapped a palm on the table. "Let's go blow off
some steam at the gym. You game?"

Iain smiled his gratitude. "I'm game. And Bryan,
thanks."

"No sweat, man."

Kani loved auditions—the chance to meet new people, the
chance to observe the variety of acting styles. She chuckled
to herself. Auditions were especially fun when she wasn't the
one auditioning. Nice to have the pressure off.

Except that there was a different kind of pressure tonight. Iain. He sat beside Robert and Robert's assistant director, conversing as an equal, fully involved in the
production. Kani had relegated herself to the background,
soothing frazzled nerves, giving pep talks and recruiting
backstage help, but she wished she knew what Robert and
Iain were discussing. The performers had already been
reading scenes for over two hours when Robert had told
everyone to take a break, then he, Iain and the assistant director had huddled.

She was entitled to be in on the conversation. *So go,* she
urged herself. *They didn't ask me,* a petty little voice answered. *Coward.* Kani threw her hands in the air. Even her
blasted conscience was criticizing her now.

It was true, though. She *was* being a coward. She hadn't
said more than ten words to Iain in four days, and she didn't
know how to share in a discussion with him now, even a

business one. Something had to give. Undoubtedly it was going to have to be her.

She drew in a deep breath and was on her way to join the trio when a young woman strolled into the theater. Of elegant posture and long, lean lines, she was the kind of woman who drew the eye instantly, who would be mesmerizing to watch on stage. Unfortunately there wasn't a part in this production for someone of her age and stature. Kani moved toward her.

"Hi," Kani said, promptly revising her opinion. This wasn't a grown woman; she was barely out of high school, maybe not even that. "I'm Kani Warner."

"Corinne."

"Is this your first time at Ramshackle?"

The young woman's green eyes observed everything, everyone. "Yes. First time in San Francisco."

"Where'd you come from?"

"New York."

Kani smiled. "That's a turnabout. Usually everyone leaves here for there. In the theater business, anyway."

"I saw the audition notice outside."

"I'm sorry, Corinne. There aren't any parts suitable for you." Kani watched her shoulders slump. "Plenty of need for backstage help, if you're interested."

"I . . . I haven't had any experience."

"No problem. We train. We just don't pay."

Corinne finally looked at Kani. "That's okay. When do I start?"

"Whoa! I love your enthusiasm, but we won't open for almost seven weeks."

"You mean I can't do anything until then?"

"Not unless you want to help build the set."

"Yes! Yes, I'd love to. And anything else you need."

Kani eyed her curiously. Something didn't fit. Perfect posture and perfect diction—okay, pretty theatrical, both. But ragged, unwashed clothes and the gleam of desperation in her eyes? What was her story? "Would you like to work as the prompter during rehearsals? Are your nights free?''

''I haven't found a job yet. I'm *completely* free.''

''We'll talk more after auditions are over, Corinne. Have a seat and watch, if you'd like.''

Kani got her settled in a seat just as auditions began again, and she frowned at missing her chance to join the conversation with Iain and Robert. Half an hour later, they called it quits for the night and announced callbacks for the following evening. She checked locks and turned off lights as the three men concluded their discussion, then she waited for them to exit before flipping the last light switch and heading for the lobby.

Iain awaited her. So did Corinne, and she was staring at Iain with stars in her eyes. Kani approached the girl. She didn't know why she felt uncomfortable with the way Corinne stared at Iain, especially since Iain's expression reflected discomfort. ''Corinne,'' Kani said into the tense silence, ''we won't need you to start prompting for several weeks.''

Dismay flashed across the girl's face. ''Couldn't I be here, anyway—so I can get to know everyone and they can get to know me? Remember, I want to help with the set, too.''

Kani dug out a rehearsal schedule and passed it to Corinne. ''Feel free to come. I'll let you know about the set. This is Iain MacKenzie, by the way. He's the playwright.''

Corinne stuck her arm straight out; Iain had no choice but to shake hands with her. When his glance lifted to her face, he was astounded at her expression. Women had occasionally been attracted to him just for his looks, an occurrence that was baffling to him because he'd never considered himself out of the ordinary, but this girl's reaction to him was positively...*adoring*.

''We'll see you tomorrow night,'' Kani said, drawing Corinne's gaze.

''Great.'' The girl grinned, then sent an even wider smile Iain's way before hefting her backpack over her shoulder and walking out of the building.

"Trouble," Iain said, shaking his head.

"I hope she has a place to stay," Kani mused.

Corinne was waiting on the doorstep of the theater the next night, and the next, her cheek pillowed against the backpack in her lap as she slept. Kani's sympathies having forever run toward stray animals and runaway children, she was attuned more to Corinne's actions than her words.

When Kani asked her if she was all right, Corinne answered a cheerful yes. But Kani noticed that Corinne spent a lot of time in the rest room after they first unlocked the door, and she always emerged with a clean face, damp hair and smelling of soap and toothpaste. She alternated sweat-shirts but her clothes were otherwise unchanged.

Without a specific job to do yet, Corinne just planted herself where she could observe everyone. The only people she spoke to were Kani and Iain, much to his chagrin. Kani knew he was uncomfortable that Corinne had singled him out, but they didn't discuss it. They hadn't discussed much of anything for days.

Clipboard in hand, Kani dropped into a seat beside Corinne as everyone else continued the read-through of the script. She passed the board and a pen to the teenager. "Since you're part of the team, we'll need some data on you. Full name, address, phone."

Corinne stared at the blank paper, then at Kani.

"Do you have a place to stay?" Kani asked gently.

The girl's lips pursed as she shook her head.

"Where have you been staying?"

She shrugged a shoulder defensively. "The bus station."

"Why?"

She fidgeted with the fastener on the clipboard, snapping it nervously. "My boyfriend kind of left me here."

"Did you come from New York together?"

"Yeah."

"Do you have any money?"

"Not much. I've been applying for jobs, but without an address or phone number they won't even talk to me."

"What about your parents, Corinne?"

A final loud snap of the clip substituted for words.

The sigh Kani heaved inwardly could have won awards. "I want you to come home with me. You can stay with us until—well, for a while, anyway."

Kani watched Corinne's gaze shift to Iain briefly.

"I won't be any trouble," Corinne said.

I don't think Iain will agree with that, Kani thought, caught between amusement and resignation.

Walking home that night, Corinne insinuated herself between Kani and Iain, which wouldn't normally have bothered Kani since she wanted to avoid him, anyway. But the mere fact that this *child* obviously had a crush on Iain made her fume.

Even though she no longer laid claim to him.

It had been a lonely and painful time since the night in her bedroom. She wished they could go back, not take the risk they'd both known they were taking by watching television together from her bed. She wanted a chance to start slowly with him, not to pressure him, not to expect so much from him. But that chance was gone. Killed. Dead and buried.

Kani helped Corinne settle in a bedroom across the hall from hers, gave her clean towels, and told her to come downstairs after her shower for a snack. In the kitchen, Iain awaited her.

"I can't believe you fell for that," he said without preamble. At the theater he had merely raised his brows when Kani announced that Corinne would be coming home with them.

"Fell for what?" She opened a can of tuna and began mixing it with mayonnaise.

"That act of hers. I see what your brother means about you now."

"Do you?" Her voice seemed nonchalant. "Do you think she lied when she said she needed a place to stay?"

"Maybe not, but—"

"Do you think she lied when she said she didn't have any money?"

"Probably not, but—"

Kani faced him, eyes blazing. "Maybe her story wasn't quite true. But this much I do know—she's known better times. Her jeans are ragged, but they're designer. Her shoes are dirty, but they're name brand. And while I've never had the privilege of having one myself, that's a hundred-dollar haircut she's got.

"Now, the mere fact the cut's new enough for me to notice the quality means she hasn't been gone from home for too long. Do you want it on your conscience if she's living at the bus station, or in a park, or wherever else runaways stay these days, and she's raped, or forced into prostitution? I know I don't.

"So I offered her a place to stay, a chance to get clean, some food in her stomach. So what? What's the worst that can happen? She might leave with a VCR under her arm to pawn? *So what?* The things of value in this house are human. And animal," she added as Gypsy wove in and out of her legs, her nose in the air sniffing the scent of tuna. "Give the kid a break."

Having always looked out only for himself, Iain was humbled by Kani's humanity. In Mexico he had prayed to God to let him rise to Kani's level, not bring her down to his. He hadn't done that to her. Thank God she'd stayed innocent.

"And what am I supposed to do about her obvious infatuation?" he asked Kani.

"Oh, you're pretty damn good at squelching infatuation. I have every confidence you can do it."

That hurt. That really, really hurt. Even though he deserved it, to hear her say it cut more deeply than anything anyone had ever said to him. Maybe he should move in with Wes and Julia, after all. Maybe—

"That felt great!" Corinne said as she joined them. She was wearing a bathrobe of Kani's; her chin-length blond hair hung wet and straight. Clean, she looked even younger.

"How old are you?" Iain asked her.

"Eighteen."

The answer came too fast, he thought. His expression showed his disbelief. "Why are you on your own?"

"Iain, drop it," Kani said. "Let her eat in peace. Here, Corinne. Do you want a soft drink with that?"

"I'd kill for a glass of milk," she said, grinning. "My mother'd die if she heard me say that."

Kani smiled and poured a glass, passing it to the girl, then taking a seat across from her. "It's amazing how good it tastes when you can't have it."

"Forbidden fruit," Iain said, also taking a seat. "The expectation is always better than the fulfillment."

And sometimes the fulfillment exceeds the expectation, Kani thought. *Like making love with you, Iain MacKenzie. Dammit! Why can't I stop thinking about it?*

"Corinne," Kani said, ramming her wayward thoughts into the back of her mind, "we do expect you to earn your keep."

"Just tell me what to do." She chewed quickly, as if she hadn't eaten for days. Twice she refilled her glass as they talked.

"Keep your own room clean. You and I share a bathroom, so I expect it to be kept orderly and clean, as well. Everybody's on their own for most meals, so the kitchen's open to you to cook, but clean up after yourself. You can use the washer and dryer. I also have some clothes you can borrow, if you don't mind hand-me-downs. The vacuum cleaner is in the pantry. Feel free to use it when you see a need."

"How long can I stay?"

"I won't give you a time frame. It depends on how well everything's working out. It's important that we all get along. If we don't, then things have to change."

"How long will you be here?" Corinne asked Iain.

"My status is the same as yours."

"So you and she—" she cocked her head toward Kani "—don't, um, aren't, um—"

"An item? No. I'm a guest, same as you. And her name is Kani."

Corinne smiled broadly, wadded her napkin and tossed it on her plate. "Great! Well, I think I'll go to bed, if you don't mind. I'm really tired."

"Spoiled little brat," Iain muttered when she'd gone.

"Yeah." Kani smiled, pleased that Iain wasn't happy about the girl's infatuation. He was also really rather cute when he was annoyed. "There's intelligence there, though, and a refreshing boldness. I think she'll be fun to have around until we can persuade her to go home to her mother."

"You think we can?"

"I have my doubts about *you,* but I think *I* can. And I think Bryan probably *will.*"

"Has a bit of success with runaways, does he?"

"Let's just say he likes his space. If I take in too many people at once, he finds solutions for them."

"The more I know him, the better I like him."

They sat in awkward silence for a few seconds, then Iain drew a deep breath. "I'm sorry, Kani."

She acted on instinct, some intuition that turned off her logic and turned on just her need, that told her if she didn't accept his apology and begin to make amends right now, she'd never get the chance again. She spoke softly to him. "You know what I really regret about the other night?"

"Tell me."

She swung a leg across him and sat in his lap, facing him, inching forward with maddening slowness. She'd taken him completely by surprise, that much she could tell, and she reveled in it. Her hands threaded his hair, cupped his head, and pulled him to within an inch of her mouth.

"We didn't even kiss." She closed the gap and pressed her lips to his, feeling the familiar lightning bolt of desire shoot through her, into him, and back again. She caught his groan in her open mouth, trapped her name called out in desperation between their tongues, felt his body harden at the vee of her legs, gloried in the hot embrace of his arms as they pulled her even closer to him. She was playing with fire; she acknowledged it and let it happen. Because the fire was so much better than the ice she lived with otherwise.

She pulled away from the vortex she was spinning into, breathing hard, hardly breathing. She stared into his eyes, those beautiful turquoise eyes with those sexy, sleepy lids, as she slowly backed off him. When she stood between his knees, he started to speak; she pressed her thumb to his lips and brushed it back and forth. Her words came with a quaver. "There. One less regret."

He sucked her thumb into his mouth and bit the pad, then pulled her hand away, crushing it in his. "What's this mean, Kani? You have to tell me where I stand."

She walked away, but then stopped, turning around to look at him. "I wish I knew, Iain."

Iain took his coffee mug into the backyard to enjoy the crisp Monday morning. He'd been awakened at seven when Kani knocked on his bedroom door and asked if he wanted to go to the gym with her. He would have preferred to go with Bryan later because he got a better workout pushing himself to keep up with the power lifter, but Iain also didn't want to hurt his fragile new beginning with Kani. So he'd gone, and he felt good now, well exercised and invigorated.

"'Morning," Bryan said, joining him after a few minutes, a steaming mug in hand. "What's Kani doing home? Is she sick?"

"I didn't know she was home. I left her at the gym over half an hour ago. Are you sure it's Kani?"

"Who else would be in the shower?"

"Ah." Iain smiled wryly. "So you don't know about your new houseguest yet."

The mug jerked to a stop halfway to Bryan's mouth. "She didn't."

"She did."

Bryan's mouth quirked, an expression registering both annoyance and resignation. "Where'd she find this one?"

"At the theater. A runaway."

"Boy or girl?"

"Girl. Corinne. Last name unknown. Address unknown. She says her boyfriend dumped her, left her on her own without any money after they'd driven here from New York."

"I gather you don't believe her."

Iain shrugged. "I suppose it's a credible enough story. She, uh, she seems to have formed an instant attraction, unfortunately, to me."

Bryan chuckled. "How old is this girl?"

"She says eighteen. I'd say a year or two younger."

"So that makes you, what? A father figure?"

"Bite your tongue."

Laughing, Bryan slapped Iain's knee. "So how're you going to handle—?"

"Iain?" Corinne called his name as she opened the back door.

He sighed melodramatically. "That's Mr. MacKenzie to you, brat," he muttered low, drawing Bryan's amused look. "Out here, Corinne," he called.

She smiled as she spotted him, then hopped down the stairs, her long, slender legs fully revealed by the shorts she'd squeezed into. "Isn't it a great day?"

Iain shrugged in reply as Bryan stood and offered his hand. "I'm Bryan Warner."

"Hi." She shook his hand cautiously. "You're Kani's brother."

"Yes."

She squirmed beneath his inspection, jumping when he took her chin between his thumb and forefinger and tilted her face toward him. She gave him her fiercest scowl but otherwise held still for the appraisal. When he released her, she almost growled her words at him. "I don't need a sugar daddy."

Iain shifted in his chair to see Bryan's reaction. He merely lifted an amused brow.

"And I don't date older—*old* men."

The left side of Bryan's mouth twitched upward.

"And I'm saving myself for marriage, so don't bother me."

Bryan laughed outright. "Don't worry, little girl. I don't molest children."

Her back stiffened. "I'm eighteen."

"Right."

The phone rang, and Corinne hurried into the house. Iain was still laughing over the exchange. "Guess I look younger than you, man. She doesn't consider *me* old."

Bryan grinned. "An insulting child, but an enlightening encounter."

"How so?"

"She wears green contact lenses, dark enough to camouflage her real color. And she probably hasn't been physically abused." At Iain's questioning expression, he said, "She jumped in surprise when I touched her, but she didn't flinch. Says a lot."

"I figured I'd check out her backpack for ID as soon as I got the chance," Iain said.

"I'll handle it," Bryan told him. "I admit I've learned to trust Kani's instincts. She's brought home at least a hundred kids over the past ten years, and nothing's happened because of it. But I check them all out as much as possible."

"I'm really uncomfortable with this kid—"

Corinne stuck her head out the door, interrupting Iain's words. "Phone for you, Iain. A Mr. Bellanger."

"My old boss," Iain said softly to Bryan as he stood.

"Use the phone in my office."

"Thanks, I will."

Iain gave Corinne a wide berth as he mounted the stairs two at a time. He heard Bryan ask if she could cook.

"Kind of," she replied.

"Meaning what? You can boil water?"

"If you want breakfast, just say so. You don't have to insult me to get me to work."

As he rounded the corner of the kitchen, Iain glanced back at Bryan, catching the smile Bryan gave her for her impertinence.

"Actually I was thinking we'd cook together—breakfast for three. You game?"

"Just keep your hands to yourself."

"That I can promise, little girl."

In the end, Bryan and Iain only did the dishes because Corinne pulled together a credibly good meal of eggs, ham, cantaloupe and toast. When they heard the vacuum cleaner turn on upstairs, Iain turned to Bryan, who was wiping down the kitchen counter.

"It seems my sterling writing talents are missed."

"They want you back?" Bryan asked.

"Immediately. After I talked with Gayle on Friday, she went to the producer to tell him what Kani and Julia had said about the plot changes. Apparently there were a lot of phone calls to the network affiliates, as well. Anyway, they're *very* anxious for me to return."

"What will you do?"

Iain grinned. "Use the power they've given me, of course. I'm getting a substantial salary increase, back pay for my forced 'vacation,' and I can work from here. They'll pay for another phone line, modem and a fax machine. I'll have conference calls with the other writers and write from here, then transmit down to them. I told them I'd give them six months, then we'd negotiate a new contract."

Bryan whistled. "Good job, man. Sounds like you got 'em where you want 'em. Are you going to tell Kani?"

"I don't think so, not yet. Anything I write won't show up on televised episodes for a month or so. And frankly, she's a good source for reaction. She and Julia both. If I tell her, her critique won't be nearly as helpful."

"She'll give it to you straight."

Iain shook his head thoughtfully. "I don't think so. I think her reaction would be tempered by my involvement. She'd pull her punches a little."

"Maybe. She wouldn't want to hurt your feelings."

"Exactly. I couldn't have asked for a better work situation." He eyed Bryan curiously. "Or would you rather move out now that I can afford it?"

Bryan leaned against the counter, crossing his arms over his chest. "I'm enjoying your company. Why don't you stay? And let me take care of the extra phone line. I've—"

"Got contacts?" Iain completed the sentence. Life was definitely looking up.

"You're in a good mood," Kani said to Iain that night after they'd arrived at the theater. Corinne had been assigned the job of production secretary, requiring that she sit beside Robert and write down the actors' moves—the blocking—on a copy of the script. Iain had suggested the job as a way to keep her from following him around, and Kani agreed it was a good idea.

She and Iain were in the scene shop alone, insulated from the stage and performers, as they looked at a scale model the set designer had built of the set for *Journeys*.

Iain watched Kani examine each detail of the model. He *was* in a good mood, he realized. She'd kissed him last night, and it had given him hope. He'd gotten his job back today—on his own terms—and that had given him security. If only Corinne didn't demand so much of him—

"Iain?" Kani said, watching him closely. "What's going on?"

He captured a loose lock of silky hair and rubbed it between his fingers. He felt her tension rise until he let go, then shoved both hands into his back pockets.

"I'm relaxed for the first time since Mazatlán," he admitted.

"Why?"

His shoulders lifted in a quick shrug. "Everything's under control."

She smiled lopsidedly. "Everything? I'm envious."

"Everything except you," he corrected.

She stepped closer to him and ran a finger down the buttons of his shirt, obviously accepting his unspoken chal-

age. "Now why would you want me under control? Then
u'd be so relaxed you'd slip into complacency."

His breath snagged as her finger circled the bottom but-
n, then hooked into his waistband and tugged. "Com-
acency," he said, choking, "would be the kiss of death, I
gree."

At the word "kiss," Kani's gaze focused on Iain's mouth;
r tongue darted out to moisten her lips.

"Is this for real, or are you teasing?" he asked as his body
sponded to her nearness, the desire on her face and the
emories in his heart. He sucked in a breath as her hand
ifted down the hardness pressing against the buttoned
acket of his jeans.

He cupped her bottom and lifted her, closing his eyes
iefly as her legs wound around his hips. Setting her on a
unter, he shoved her T-shirt up, unclasped the front hook
the scrap of silk she called a bra, and pulled an erect nip-
e into his mouth, groaning with her as her head fell back,
en dropped forward to rest on his. Her hands pressed his
eeks, holding him to her as he suckled and savored, her
umbs stroking the corners of his mouth and catching his
ngue as it laved her taut flesh—a double dose of erotic
ensation.

He cupped a hand at the vee of her legs and felt her
ampness through the denim. It wouldn't take much con-
ct to send her soaring, he knew. Lord, she was the most
sponsive woman he'd ever known, hot and open and giv-
g.

And if he satisfied her here and now? What of him? An-
ther bout of frustration that would take five cold showers
calm? He leaned back and lowered her T-shirt. "Will you
ome to me tonight, Kani?"

Ten

Her eyes glittered with a wildness he'd never seen. Her breath came short and shallow. If he touched her again she'd be lost. He stepped away and watched her cool down, which did nothing for the ache in his loins. If anything, the pounding intensified. She slid off the counter, walked a few steps, then leaned her hands on a table. Carefully she rehooked her bra and straightened her clothes.

"I'm sorry," she said, her back to him. "I didn't mean for that to happen."

"I figured that. But knowing doesn't make it easier."

"I can't let myself get involved with you again." Her voice dropped to a whisper. "And I can't seem to help myself."

He laid a hand on her shoulder for a moment. "Why can't we enjoy the pleasure, Average? What harm would come of it?"

She turned around slowly. "Can you handle the truth, Iain?"

"Enlighten me."

She drew a deep breath, creating a fortress around herself. "More than anything I want someone who will make a
lifetime commitment to me. *And you're not it.*"

"What about Mazatlán? What was that about?" He held
himself rigid, afraid of her answer.

"My last fling," she said matter-of-factly, as if trying to
believe it herself.

"Is there no hope for us?" he asked, forcing words past
a lump in his throat.

"Let's be friends," she said. "We've got a long way to go
in the play. Let's just put the memories aside and start
fresh."

"Can you do that?"

"I have to do that. Sex isn't everything."

"It counts for a helluva lot, Kani. Sometimes it's everything."

"If you can only communicate through sex, it isn't a
healthy relationship. I need someone to talk with, someone
to share dreams and problems with."

"And I deal with problems alone," he said.

She sighed. "I know."

Iain crossed his arms over his chest and contemplated her.
"I'll give it a try, this friendship business."

"You will? You won't pressure me physically?"

"Seems to me you've been the one instigating everything
that's happened between us recently. Ah, you have the grace
to blush. I'll keep my hands off you, but you have to promise me something."

"What?" Wariness crept into her voice.

"That if and when you want to resume a physical relationship, you won't let pride stop you."

She nodded her head several times.

"Good." He turned, took a few steps, then turned back.
"We didn't kiss. I don't want to leave you regretful again.
Shall we—?"

"No!"

He chuckled at the look of horror on her face. How long
can you hold out, my sexy Kani? he thought. How long?

*   *   *

Iain hung up the phone and stretched. It wasn't unusual for him to spend several hours a day in conference calls with the writing team before he settled down to write script. Today had begun and ended with calls, and his muscles screamed at the enforced confinement.

He glanced at the clock; Kani would be home from work soon. No time for a hot shower to loosen the tightness in his body before he made dinner. He straightened his desk top, filed papers, and covered his computer before wandering into the kitchen.

The refrigerator was relatively full for a change, because *he'd* done the shopping. No one else seemed to care whether there was food in the house, so he'd taken on the responsibility of shopping and cooking. He set salad makings on the counter beside the refrigerator, assuming Corinne would show up and knowing he'd be a captive audience for the time it took to prepare dinner. He'd waited several evenings for her to offer assistance, but she'd merely leaned against the counter and watched him work as she talked. Finally he'd flipped a head of lettuce to her. She'd tossed the lettuce in the air a few times, grinned at him, then had fixed the salad, thus beginning a nightly pattern.

He dumped rice and water into a casserole and set it in the microwave as he heard Corinne scurry down the stairs. From the refrigerator he pulled out the ingredients for teriyaki chicken stir-fry.

"Hi! Rough day?" she asked as she retrieved the salad bowl from the cupboard beside the refrigerator.

"Not bad."

"What exactly do you *do,* Iain?"

"I write."

"You write what?"

He put chicken breasts and a few vegetables on the counter. "I'm a playwright, remember?"

She stood staring at him, the bowl clutched to her stomach. "I haven't met a playwright before, but just as a wild guess, I'd say most of them don't spend a good part of the day on the telephone."

Iain gave her a cool glance, and she grinned.

"Just a guess," she repeated. "I wasn't snooping. I heard voices coming from your room and couldn't figure out who you had in there."

"So you listened."

"Only long enough to know you were alone." She pulled out a wooden cutting board and knife, then moved the salad fixings closer to her. "Have you ever been married?"

"Nope." Iain set another cutting board on the counter opposite her. "Have you?"

Corinne laughed. "Nope," she mimicked. "Got any kids?"

"Nope." He kept the smile off his face as he continued the game. When she wasn't being too pushy or too teen-agerish, she was reasonably likable. "You?"

"Nope. Have you ever been in love?"

"Nope."

"Never? Not even a little bit?"

He contemplated the clammy chicken breast he'd just plopped onto the board. "Maybe a little bit, when I was too young to know better."

"You don't believe in love?"

"Do you?" he asked.

"Of course."

"Good luck." She'd stopped slicing tomatoes, and he could feel her gaze on him, but he continued to cut the chicken into strips.

"Why do you say that?" she asked.

"Seems to me, Corinne, that you should have learned the hard way already. Didn't your boyfriend dump you here? My guess is you started off with stars in your eyes, and look what happened."

She shrugged. "He wasn't all that great anyway. We fought a lot. I'll find someone more mature next time."

Iain's mouth quirked. "You told Bryan you didn't like older men."

"Older doesn't necessarily mean mature."

He glanced up at her, knife in hand. "Finally, words o
wisdom."

She straightened, knife in hand. "Finally, words o
praise."

They stared at each other for a minute before returning t
their individual tasks.

"Why don't you like me?" she asked.

"I like you."

"You don't show it."

"I'm not a teenager."

"Yes, I know. You're a mature man. *I* like *you*."

Iain set his knife aside when he realized he was missing re
bell peppers. "I can't imagine why," he said, leaning int
the refrigerator and pulling open the vegetable drawer.

From behind him, Corinne wrapped her arms around hi
waist and leaned her cheek against his back. "I don't knov
either. I—"

Iain jerked upright, shoving her arms down. Spinning, h
caught her by the shoulders and pushed her a full foot awa

"What's going on here?"

Kani's voice, cool and controlled, blanketed the room.

"Nothing," Corinne said calmly. She moved to th
counter, turning her back on both Kani and Iain as sh
picked up her knife again and busily chopped cucumber.

Iain watched Kani's gaze flicker from Corinne's taut bod
to his own. His teeth clenched; his jaw tightened. *Why now
Just when we'd been building trust—dammit! Damn the gir
and her infatuation.*

Silently fuming, he finished slicing vegetables. Corinne se
the completed salad in the refrigerator and left. Kani set th
table.

The oil in the pan sizzled as Iain dropped in the ingredi
ents a few at a time. He felt Kani's presence, her unspoke
questions. "I didn't do anything to encourage her," he sai
finally.

"I didn't think you did."

He turned his head toward her. She was leaning against the counter, one ankle resting over the other, her arms crossed. Everything in her body language indicated she was willing to be convinced of her own words.

"This isn't my home. I can't ask her to leave," he said.

Her brows arched. "If you're saying that *I* should, think again. She needs to be here right now. I'm surprised you can't handle her. She's just a kid."

"I've been civil to her because it's important to you."

"I don't care if things are a little antagonistic between you, if that's what it takes to discourage her, but I don't want her hurt."

Iain's mouth twitched. "I see. It's okay for me to be hurt, but let's save the kid's pride."

Kani pushed away from the counter and moved to stand beside him, deciding it was time to show her faith in him. "She still has illusions."

"Unlike you?"

She surprised him with a smile. "Mine are still intact. It takes a lot to shatter mine altogether."

Iain stared at her before trailing his fingertips down her cheek, stopping at her jaw. "I really didn't do anything to prompt her to grab me like that."

"I believe you, Iain."

"Do you? Honestly?"

"Honestly." She tried not to show how his touch affected her, but his intense scrutiny led her to think she had somehow revealed what she sought to trap inside. She saw his relief that she believed him without question. She was disappointed when he returned to the task of stir-frying, thus losing the contact of his skin against hers.

"Would you tell me about John Q?" he said as she moved away from him.

The microwave *beeped,* indicating the rice was done. Kani pulled out the casserole dish and set it on the table. "Who told you about *him?*"

"Your brother said his name but little else. I only know
he was your last boyfriend, that he was an actor with a big
ego, and that he went to New York."

"That about sums it up."

"Were you in love with him?"

The question surprised her because he rarely asked anything so personal. She had decided he didn't want to give her
the right to ask anything personal in return. "I thought I
was in love with him."

"He hurt you."

"Yes. Yes, he did."

Iain thought about her words as he poured the main
course into a large serving bowl. "Yet you still trust people."

She waited until he stopped moving and turned to her.
Her voice was soft and full of understanding. "He was only
one person, Iain. He represented himself, not the entire
population."

"How do you let go of it, Kani? How can it not color
your outlook?"

"Because I see the glass as half-full, not half-empty. I always have and I always will. You should try it sometime,
Iain. It's a lot less exhausting."

"Maybe if you'd lived my life, you wouldn't be so quick
to offer advice."

"Maybe I wouldn't. I'll tell you what—any time you feel
like enlightening me about your life, I'll be happy to listen.
I promise not to offer unsolicited advice. I'd be curious to
know what's made you decide that marriage would be like
prison and fatherhood a curse."

Iain's gaze moved past Kani to the doorway, where Corinne stood watching them, listening to their words.

"I thought...I smelled dinner," she said. "I didn't mean
to eavesdrop."

"It's all right," Kani said. "Bring the salad, please."

"I...I'm still welcome?"

"Of course you are."

"Iain?" Corinne pressed.

He nodded once but concentrated on serving himself.

Corinne met Kani's gaze before shrugging off the tension and providing her usual dinnertime chatter. Kani, for one, was grateful.

"And don't call me brat," Corinne ordered Iain from the back seat of his car.

Kani shook her head in bemusement. She never would have believed it of Iain, that he could bicker. Yet he and Corinne sparred constantly. Kani knew Iain was frustrated by Corinne's attention, her almost dogged devotion to him, but Kani also recognized flirtation when she saw it. Corinne was just testing her wiles as a girl hovering on the brink of womanhood was wont to do, especially if, subconsciously, she felt safe with the man. Corinne wasn't exactly in constant pursuit of him; she was just *always there,* near him.

And it drove Iain crazy.

"I call it as I see it," Iain said to the girl after a quick glance in the rearview mirror. "You've said *Journeys* is your first experience working in theater. You can't order the director around. Your job is to do what's asked of you, not to offer advice to a thirty-year veteran of the stage."

The ten-minute drive from home to Wes and Julia's house seemed endless, Kani thought, both amused and exhausted by Iain's and Corinne's lively discussion. They'd started exchanging verbal gunfire the minute their seat belts were buckled and hadn't paused to draw breath since.

"He may have thirty years of experience, but he's got Edwina's character all wrong," Corinne said with assurance.

"*I* don't think so, and I wrote the play," he returned, slowing down to look for a parking space.

"When you wrote the play, did you picture anyone playing Edwina's part?"

Kani heard a fractional hesitation in his voice when he answered, "No."

"Liar. You must have. I'll tell you who *I* see. Helen Hunt."

Iain snorted. "She's like twenty years too old," he said unconsciously regressing into teenage speech patterns.

"Not at her age *now*. When she was younger. I saw her i a play—it was the first play I'd ever seen, as a matter o fact—when I was seven. She was incredible. And *that's* wh your Edwina character is."

"If you saw her on stage, she was playing a part. The pai was probably similar to Edwina, ergo, your connection Great timing," he said as a car pulled out two houses fron Wes and Julia's.

Corinne frowned, obviously unwilling to yield to Iain' logic. Kani finally ventured a comment. "He's right, yo know."

"Maybe." She crossed her arms and glared out the sid window as Iain parked the car.

"Brat," Iain said.

"Philistine."

Kani laughed as she opened the car door and climbed ou "Truce, you two. I knew I should have left one of you home."

"He started it," Corinne said.

Kani lifted her brows at Iain in a blatant reminder that h was an adult; he raised his hands in capitulation. She looke from one to the other. "Now, I want you both to behave o I'll send you to your rooms without dessert."

"Yes, Mother," they replied in unison, startling all thre of them into laughter.

Kani was grateful for the diversion the bickering duo of fered. It had been a difficult couple of weeks for her. Sh and Iain tiptoed around each other, avoiding contact—sor of—making an effort toward friendship—sort of. She wen to the gym early, and he went later in the day, often wit Bryan; otherwise she had no idea how he spent his day, an she was determined not to ask him. He wasn't helping buil the set, and Corinne, for all her offers of help, showed litt interest, as well. The only time Corinne went to the theate as at night for rehearsals, when Iain would also be there. he didn't look for a job, although she did keep the house potlessly clean.

Kani didn't know what to think of Corinne, whether to be ealous of her or to feel sorry for her. The few conversaons they'd had resulted in no new revelations from the enager. She seemed absurdly content.

If only I could be so content, Kani thought, waiting for ain to open the trunk of the car, where he'd put a bowl of uit salad. She missed him—his dry wit, his passion. They habited the same house but lived almost separate lives. If ey hadn't had rehearsals every night, they would probaly rarely see each other. They sought friendship with the eed of a beachgoer at the ocean in winter—first testing the aters with a toe, then taking a step and getting accusomed before moving farther. Kani figured they were in up their knees.

But every so often she caught Iain watching her with a leak sort of hunger, and she knew it was an effort for him stay away, as well. It was for the best, she decided. Her motions floated in a limbo she'd never have guessed exted, drifting between love and hate.

You can count on me, Iain, she'd said mentally, over and ver, trying to tell him telepathically what she dared not utr aloud. In her saner moments, she acknowledged the fulity of their relationship, if what they shared could be alled that. In her less rational moments, she dreamed of white picket fences and turquoise-eyed babies.

Fortunately, sanity prevailed more often than not.

Iain leaned past Kani, brushing her arm with his as he icked up the bowl and slammed the trunk shut.

"Sorry," he said, his gaze connecting with hers.

For a moment, a very brief moment, Kani thought he was oing to kiss her. She held her breath, unwilling to let go of he closeness.

He leaned toward her.

"I've already rung the bell," Corinne called, oblivious to he emotion hanging heavy between Kani and Iain.

They stepped back at the same time. Kani stumbled ove
the curb; Iain caught her before she fell.

"Thanks. I . . . thanks," she said, her body filled with
meteor shower of reaction.

"My fault," he said, releasing her as soon as she steppe
onto the sidewalk. Her lemony scent filtered past the arom
of strawberries, bananas and pineapple in the bowl he wa
holding. He wanted to heave it aside and devour her mouth

"Welcome" they heard Julia say to Corinne. Reluctantl
they climbed the stairs to where Julia awaited them, bab
Jeremy balanced on her hip.

Kani smiled at the ebony-haired infant and held her hand
out to him. He threw himself at her, always glad to play wit
someone new. "He is absolutely the most well-adjuste
child," Kani said to Julia as she cuddled him while fendin
off his efforts to grab the silver fish dangling from her lef
ear.

"Well, of course he is," Wes said, coming up behind hi
wife. "He hangs out with about a trillion people every week
one of the advantages of being part of a big family."

Gnawing on a teething biscuit, Jeremy bounced in
springy chair hung in the doorway that separated the kitche
from the dining room as the adults enjoyed lasagna, garli
bread, tossed salad and then the fruit salad for dessert.

After dinner, they intended to discuss the media blitz fo
the play; during dinner, Jeremy held center stage with hi
energetic bouncing, bubble blowing and baby sounds. Iai
admired the way Wes simultaneously interacted with his son
flattered his wife, ate dinner and socialized freely with hi
guests. Dinner became an event both satisfying and invig
orating.

"I gave the maid the night off," Julia said, tongue-in
cheek. "If everyone will help clear, I'll put the dishes in t
soak."

"Let's just do the dishes, Julia," Kani said. "Lasagna'
gruesome to clean up. Corinne and I will help."

"Hey," the teenager argued, "why is it that the women always do the dishes?"

Julia smiled, a plate in each hand. "In this case, because Wes made dinner and Iain made dessert. Besides, Jeremy needs his diaper changed. Iain can help Wes."

"No way," Iain said. "I'd rather do dishes."

Wes released Jeremy from his straps and peered into his shorts. "He's only wet, Iain."

"I'll help in the kitchen. Thanks, anyway, pal."

Wes left with the baby, and Julia pushed Iain back into the living room. "We want to girl talk. Keep Wes company when he's done with the cutie. Brandy's in the hutch," she called as he left the kitchen.

He ignored the brandy; instead, he stood at the living room window contemplating the sky.

It was Sunday. The end of another long week, their only rehearsal-free night. He should have gone out, given Kani the impression of having a date. Gotten away from Corinne for a night!

He still didn't know what to make of the teenager. She followed him around like a toddler having discovered an older sibling, looked at him as if he was some sort of idol, badgered him with questions. She was impertinent and gregarious, and undaunted by his constant rejection. He growled at her to leave him the hell alone. Nuisance. Brat. *Still* she dogged him. And he'd about reached his breaking point.

How the hell had his life become so complicated? A few months ago, he'd been living in relative peace, with money in the bank, a steady job and no dark-haired woman to disrupt his sleep and invade his daydreams. Nor had there been a confused teenager practicing her feminine wiles on him, making him crazy.

Women.

"See something fascinating?" Wes asked, coming up beside Iain. Jeremy yanked a jet black lock of his daddy's hair and giggled gleefully.

"Just contemplating life," Iain replied, sarcasm coating his words.

"Damned if it doesn't keep changing, right?"

"Right. My life used to be so easy, so—"

"Stagnant." Wes interjected the softly spoken word and added a telling expression.

Iain closed his eyes briefly. "Yes. I don't know which is worse."

"Yes, you do." With the utmost nonchalance, he deposited his son into Iain's hands, ignoring the way Iain's mouth dropped open in shock. "I've got to gather material for the meeting. Hang on to Jeremy for a minute, will you?"

"But...We-Wes, I don't...know..." His voice faded as he finished the sentence. "...what to do."

Wes kept walking. Iain looked at the tiny person dangling from his hands, at one bare foot crossing the other, at the dimpled knees pulled up almost level with his waist, a chubby fist jammed into a drooly mouth, the wet smile, the sparkling Linnell brown eyes—and he was lost.

Awkwardly he cuddled the little boy closer and sank into a chair. Seating Jeremy on his lap facing him, he gently bounced him up and down. He didn't say a word, didn't know what to say, but Jeremy didn't seem to expect anything of him; he just giggled and grinned, and stole Iain's heart.

Kani walked into the room to return dishes to the hutch and saw them together—the man she loved holding the bundle of delight. The room closed in around her. All she could see was the two of them, framed as if in a sepia vignette, an oval haze around them; all she could hear was the baby's laughter. Iain handled him like the finest crystal, but Jeremy demanded no such gentle treatment. He reached out to entwine his strong fingers into the fabric of Iain's shirt, pulling the garment from his pants, tugging until he could get the cloth into his mouth to press against his gums.

Iain made no move to stop him, even though a wet splotch quickly marred the front of his shirt. Then he hesitantly pressed his lips to the soft curls and breathed in the sweet baby scent.

Kani set the dishes down on the table and pushed her palm against her mouth. Iain turned his head at the sound of her quickly indrawn breath. She walked slowly toward them and fell to her knees beside the chair.

"He's beautiful," Iain said in wonder, looking from Kani's shining hair to Jeremy's perfect miniature features.

"I know."

He swallowed hard. *How could anyone leave their child? How could my mother leave me?* The words were ripped from his heart, torn from the deepest recesses of his mind, where the rejection had been relegated since he'd found out his mother wasn't dead. It had been ten long, cold years of living with that hard knowledge.

She had been the first woman to reject him but not the last. There had been two others, one before he knew of his mother's deception, one after. There would never be another. He couldn't survive it.

Iain stared into Kani's eyes, then hardened his heart against her silently offered sympathy for the trauma she could see him experiencing. Carefully he passed Jeremy to Kani. "Do you really need me at this meeting?"

"To tell the truth, even *I'm* probably not needed. Wes and Julia are just informing us what they're doing to market the play, not asking us."

"I need to get out for a while. Wes will see you get home. Okay?"

She wondered what he would do if she refused, but she knew she couldn't hold him. He was a man accustomed to plenty of space and privacy. She would give him that. "Whatever you need, Iain."

He glanced at Jeremy, who was nestled snugly against Kani, watching Iain with a serious and contemplative expression before suddenly breaking into a heart-stopping, one-tooth smile. Iain brushed his fingers through Jeremy's hair, then settled his hand along Kani's cheek.

His head moved by slow increments until his lips skimmed hers. He deepened the kiss for a moment, not letting passion take over, wanting just the contact, the warmth, the familiar taste. Then he was gone, like King Arthur vanishing into the mists of Avalon.

Another brief and shining moment gone.

A minute later, when Corinne came out of the kitchen with Julia and discovered Iain gone, she let Kani know how angry she was that Iain had left without telling her, without taking her with him. She fumed openly, shot daggers at Kani with her eyes, and heaved long-suffering sighs over and over. Finally she pushed herself out of the living room chair.

"I'm outta here," she announced and headed for the door.

Kani didn't fight her. Figuring Iain out and trying not to intrude into his privacy had taken all the fight out of her. "Do you know how to get home?"

"Like you care."

"I care," Kani said quietly as the front door closed.

Accepting a ride from Wes, Kani beat Corinne home. She busied herself straightening her bedroom until she heard the teenager return home an hour later than it should have taken her.

Kani's relief was short-lived. One home, but one still out. She resumed pacing the floor until hours later when Iain finally returned. Only then did she sleep.

Kani sat near the back of the theater the next night. Exhaustion weighed her down as if she wore five-pound weights on her wrists and ankles.

The pattern of her life had become predictable: gym, work, quick dinner, rehearsal, watch "A Time to Love," try to sleep. Layering everything was a desire for Iain that grew daily, amused exasperation over Corinne's teenage enthusiasm, and frustration over having become what amounted to an errand girl at the theater *she owned*.

Well, her situation at the theater was something she could regain control over. She stood, drew a breath and straightened her shoulders. After marching down the row of seats in front of Iain and Robert, she stopped abruptly before them. "Robert, I've assigned someone to each job, and everything's completely under control for the production. I'll be joining you during rehearsals from now on."

"That's fine, Kani," Robert said before thumbing through his notebook, effectively dismissing her.

A little at a loss, Kani sank slowly into a seat in front of Iain and stared straight ahead. After a minute, Robert moved to the stage to give notes from the previous rehearsal, and Kani felt the back of her seat being jostled repeatedly.

She gave him her profile. Her voice was sweetness and light. "Do you want something, Iain?"

"It's about time, Average."

At the use of his nickname for her, she spun around to face him. "Meaning what?"

"I was wondering just how long you were going to let everyone else run your show."

"You were? Why didn't you say anything?"

He cocked his head at her. "I didn't think you needed me to point out the obvious."

"Maybe I do need you..." She let the sentence fade into several seconds of silence before finishing it. "...to point out the obvious."

They stared at each other, sending heated messages with their eyes. Remembering. And wishing. Then Corinne plopped into the seat beside Iain.

"Hi."

Irritated at the interruption, Iain scowled at her. "You have a job. Do it."

"Open your eyes, grouch. Nobody needs me at the moment."

"Responsible people are prepared."

Corinne was undaunted. "So are Boy Scouts. So are *lovers*."

"And what would a child like you know about that?"

"Don't you know, Iain? It's what you *don't* know that kills you. Ah, I see the Great Roberto is ready to call action. I'm off."

"Hold on, brat." He grabbed her T-shirt and yanked her back. "Don't you have something to say to Kani?"

Kani had watched the interplay silently, alternately smiling and shaking her head. She glanced curiously at the girl.

Corinne looked at the floor. "I'm . . . I'm sorry for last night. For making you worry. It was . . . childish."

"Apology accepted."

The reluctant apologizer's gaze flew up to Kani's; Corinne had obviously not been expecting a simple acceptance, but a lecture instead. She grinned at Kani before flying to her place in the front row.

"Why'd you make her apologize?" Kani asked Iain. "It doesn't mean much when it isn't freely given."

"She made you worry."

"How would you know that?"

"I know you."

Her eyes became hooded. "Then maybe you'd better apologize for yourself, as well, *Hollywood*."

Did you wait up for me, Kani? He'd spent hours driving and thinking, trying to sort out all he was feeling, and not going home until he'd been exhausted. "If I say I'm sorry, will you know for what? I seem to have a lot to apologize for."

Stop. Stop being humble. Stop being gentle. I can't resist you when you're gentle. "Perhaps you could give a blanket apology to cover any and all infractions."

"I am truly, truly sorry."

Kani closed her eyes briefly at the sandpapery whisper. "Apology accepted."

They turned to watch Robert move up the aisle toward them. Iain tapped her on the shoulder. When she craned her neck to query him silently, he stuck out his hand. "Hi. My name is Iain MacKenzie."

Kani swallowed. Her hand slipped into his and caught fire. "Kani Warner. I've been wanting to meet you."

Chapter Eleven

———

Thwack. Thwack. Thwack. Kani pounded a nail neatly into a piece of molding. *How I Spent My Summer Vacation*, by Kani Warner. *Thwack.* Fell in love in exotic tropical paradise. *Thwack.* Gave in with shameless gusto to rampaging hormones. *Thwack.* Tried to fall out of love. *Thwack.* Battered down rampaging hormones. *Thwack.* Started anew: "Hi. My name is Iain MacKenzie." *Thwack.* Sealed with a sizzling handshake. *Thwack.*

What a farce, Kani thought with a twisted smile. Almost two weeks had passed since the tentative new start to their—relationship? She didn't even know how to categorize what they had. He'd started going to the gym with her again every day, the fifteen-minute walk giving them time to talk, time to offer childhood revelations, adult experiences, or discussions on any number of subjects.

But for some strange reason, Iain wanted to talk about "A Time to Love." And not only with her, but also with Julia. Every time Kani changed the subject, he would somehow bring it back to the soap opera. "What would you do if you were Carlotta?'' he would ask. ''What would you like Daniel to say to her?''

Every night after rehearsal, Iain, Corinne and Kani would stretch out on her bed and watch the taped show. It was a rowdy hour of interactive theater, with Kani and Corinne talking to the television and each other in lively debate. Corinne brought a whole new perspective to watching the program, with her teenager's point of view. And Iain was at his most relaxed and funny, except . . .

Except when he was at his most seductive. *Thwack*. The man never took his eyes off her. It was eerie, and flattering, and extremely arousing. During the walk to the gym he would watch her face as she spoke, cataloging her expressions and words. At the gym he would watch her exercise, almost paralyzing her with his fervent gaze. At rehearsal he would watch her with quiet intensity, distracting her from concentrating, and at home in her bedroom he would watch her with a kind of amused tenderness, an almost paternalistic indulgence.

Thwack. It gave her the creeps.

He seemed to find everything she said or did fascinating. Is this what Petruchio did to Kate in *The Taming of the Shrew* when he set out to kill her with kindness? He'd wooed and won the fair maiden by being excessively, *obnoxiously* kind, until she'd curbed her shrewish tongue and turned devotedly to him. What was Iain's motive? *Thwack*. Why had he stopped avoiding her? *Thwack*.

This was the beginning of a long weekend; she could sense it. She planned to fill her two days off working on the set. Today she would nail molding around windows and doorframes on the living-room-flanked-by-two-bedrooms set; tomorrow she would paint on a base coat so the scenic artist could sponge a wallpaperish look to the flats.

''Need some help?''

Thwunk. ''Ouch!'' The hammer missed the nail head and landed on her thumb as Iain came up behind her and startled her. ''Yow!'' The heavy tool dropped onto her sneaker-

overed toes. She didn't know which digit to grab first—
thumb or toe. Each screamed painfully.

Iain stared at her in bemusement before swooping her into
his arms and quickly descending the stairs to set her carefully onto a padded theater chair. "Are you all right? Anything broken?"

Kani stuck her thumb in her mouth while trying to pull off
her sneaker with the other hand.

Iain pushed her hand aside, untied the lace, and very, very
gently slid the shoe off. He ran his fingers over the top of her
foot and down each toe, waiting for a reaction. He heard her
quickly indrawn breath when he touched her big toe; his
gaze met hers.

She looked like a balky three-year-old, with her thumb in
her mouth and her brows drawn into a scowl. His shoulders shook briefly with laughter at the image, and he quickly
forced them still. They shook again. Went still. Then he gave
up, plopping onto the floor, laughing.

"You creep! I'm in pain, pain that *you* caused. How dare
you laugh at me! How dare you—"

Iain laughed harder, falling flat onto the floor and covering his face with his hands. When he finally dropped his
hands to his sides and propped himself up on his elbows, a
stupid grin on his face, he found Kani looming over him, the
hammer held high above her head.

He scrambled to a sitting position and warded her off
with a hand upraised to block the hammer's descent. "Now,
Kani—"

"Don't you 'now, Kani' me! You sneaked up on me,
scared me, *caused me pain,* then you laughed at me.
Laughed! On top of everything else you've done these past
two weeks, don't you think—"

"What else I have done?" he interrupted, cautiously
pulling his feet under him.

"Oh, you know. You know damn well what you've done.
I want it to stop. I want you to leave me alone."

He watched the hammer closely. "I haven't done anything, Kani. I haven't touched you—"

"You touch me all the time!"

His gaze shifted to her face, and he saw that she was serious. The pain in her expression wasn't coming only from her thumb and toe. He'd been trying to be her friend, but somehow he'd screwed up again. What the hell had he done? "I haven't laid a finger on you."

"Oh, you're hopeless! Hopeless. You *touch* me all the time! With your *eyes*. There are memories in your eyes when you look at me, when you smile at me as if we share a private joke. It's got to stop."

"Come on, Average—"

"And don't call me that! You have no right to call me that."

"So shoot me. Or hammer me. Whatever. Go on, try me without a hearing."

Her arm was beginning to ache; the hammer felt like an anvil. She dropped her arm a fraction, enough that he could reach up and pull the tool out of her weakening hand.

"I swear to you, Kani, that I haven't been intentionally doing anything to you. I have, in fact, been trying hard to just be your friend."

Her voice was full of quiet desperation as she sank down beside him. "How can we be?"

"I don't know. But I'm trying."

"For my sake?"

"Yes, of course. Who else's?"

"Yours, maybe?"

"Maybe so, Kani. Maybe I need to be protected from you, as well. Does that make you happy?"

She thought about it for a minute, then smiled. "Yes. Yes, I think it does." She leaned her elbows against her knees and propped her chin on her fists. "So where's your shadow?"

"Corinne? I ditched her."

"You didn't!"

"No, I didn't. God, your opinion of me is low. I came to help you work on the set. Do you think Corinne would get her hands dirty?"

"*You* haven't helped until now."

"I wasn't aware it was in my job description."

Kani rubbed her toe, easing out the last bit of ache. "It's not required of anyone, but everyone who has free time usually pitches in. You have all day free, I believe."

"How would you know? You're at work."

"*Are* you doing something important?"

"Believe it or not, I got a job."

Kani straightened in surprise. "Why didn't you tell me? What are you doing?"

He gave her half of the truth. "Wes asked me to try my hand at writing some ad copy."

"Advertising? But you write fiction."

Iain's mouth curved in a wry smile. "Wes says a wordsmith is a wordsmith. I've enjoyed it, actually."

"So why didn't you tell me?"

He shrugged. "I wanted to see how it would work out."

Kani hesitated. "In Mexico I'd decided you were a Peter Pan man—you know, the kind of man who doesn't grow up. Let me finish. Then it came to me that I was wrong, that you'd just had some bad breaks. I hold with my second conclusion. Can you freelance for Wes from Southern California?"

"Maybe. I'm not worried about supporting myself. I've been working since I was fourteen. I can find something. In the meantime, tell me what you need done here."

"How are you with tools?"

"I'm not gonna touch that line."

Kani grinned. "I've known men who couldn't use a hammer properly."

"You think I'm one of 'em?"

"Nope. In fact, I'd bet my life that *you* can."

Iain smiled and looked away, but not before Kani caught the smoldering flames in his eyes. He lifted her sneaker. "Shall we see if the slipper fits, Cinderella?"

He watched her closely for signs of discomfort as he eased the shoe onto her foot. He wanted to take her into his arms, wanted to offer her comfort and peace, then let it build into

passion and need. He wanted to go back to Mexico and re-
live the first six days they'd had together again and again.

Something extraordinary had happened the night he'd
held baby Jeremy in his arms. Suddenly marriage and a
family seemed a real possibility for him. Or at least it didn't
seem so terrifying and impossible. Maybe, just maybe, they
really could work this out. Maybe the gut-wrenching tightness, the muscle-weakening softness and the mind-
debilitating fogginess he always experienced around her
could be given a name. Maybe, just maybe, he was in love.
And maybe, just maybe, she really did love him in return.
Enough not to leave him, ever.

Maybe he *could* count on her.

Life didn't get better for Kani. It got, in fact, substan-
tially worse. She could hardly make a move without him
beside her, behind her. His glances had taken on distinctly
provocative properties as, merely by looking, he touched her
body here and there, leaving traces of fluttery sensations like
eyelash butterfly kisses as he followed a curve of shoulder
or breast or hip or thigh, stripping off clothes as if they were
mere nuisances, not real barriers to intimacy.

Work should have seemed like paradise in comparison.
Jake took one look at her, opened his mouth, then clamped
it shut against the questions he undoubtedly wanted to ask.
Kani's expression told him he would get no answers. Julia
fretted over her, badgering and trying to tease her out of her
strange mood, but nothing distracted Kani from seeing Iain
everywhere she turned, whether awake or asleep. One minute she would be talking with a customer; the next she would
think it was Iain in front of her. One minute she would be
asleep; the next she would be sitting straight up in bed, heart
pounding, trying to assuage her hunger for him with useless recriminations.

Life's full of pain, Iain. We go on, anyway. She'd said that
to him in Mexico, in one of her more lofty and philosophi-
cal moments. Now the big question: Do you believe your
own philosophy, Kani? If so, why don't you let yourself love

him for as long as he's here? Yes, there'll be pain, but you won't die from it.

It couldn't be any worse than not having him at all.

Kani was restless as she, Corinne and Iain watched "A Time to Love" together. It was Friday night, a week before the play was to open. The set was done, the actors ready. A few minor costume adjustments, a few minor lighting changes, a few instructions on keeping the movement tight and diction crisp, then they were home free. Robert Vandemere's expertise and professional expectations shone in her little theater. Yes, Ramshackle would close on a wondrous note, a high-quality production all the way around, from writing to performances. She would cherish the memory.

"You're not paying attention," Corinne chided her as the soap opera went into a commercial break.

"Sure I am."

"Then fast-forward."

"Oh. I'm sorry. I guess I *was* distracted."

"Yeah. Like the roof could have fallen on you."

"I said I was sorry," Kani snapped, wincing when even Gypsy lifted her head at the snippy tone. She tossed the remote at the girl. "Here, you take over."

Kani shot out of the room. Iain found her curled in a tight ball on the living room sofa. Except for some moonlight filtering through the sheer valances over the windows, the room was in darkness.

He sat beside her, curving his hand around her ankle. She tugged her feet under her. "What's the matter?"

"You can't help, Iain. Please, just leave me alone."

"You ask the impossible."

She burrowed her head farther beneath her arms. "If you care about me at all, you'll leave me alone."

"I want to help you."

"The only way you can help me is to love me." She lifted her head and focused on him through her pain. "Can you do that?"

He stroked a hand down her hair. "I can *make* love to you."

Why am I so unlovable? What is it about me that a man can't love? Stop it, Kani. Stop being pathetic. Grow up. Just . . . grow . . . up.

She spoke on a weary sigh. "You mean you can have sex with me. That *is* what you mean, isn't it? That's what you said in Mexico."

He just looked at her. When she tucked her head beneath her arms again, he left.

After a few minutes, she climbed the stairs slowly to her room. Corinne looked at her worriedly. "Did I do something? Did I make you mad?"

Kani dropped onto the bed, and Gypsy instantly leapt up to sit on her stomach, waiting to be scratched. "I had a bad day, that's all. I'm sorry I took it out on you."

"I thought maybe I was getting on your nerves. I seem to do that a lot. My mother. Iain. Bryan."

"I've enjoyed having you here, really, Corinne. But summer is winding down. Shouldn't you be thinking about going home, starting school?"

"Maybe."

"Have you called your mother to let her know you're safe?"

"No."

"If I had a child who was missing, I'd be living in hell all the time."

Corinne moved off the bed, but stopped in the doorway. "Did you ever think maybe she deserves it? Did you ever think maybe she wasn't such a good mother?"

Kani rose up on her elbows and looked over Gypsy's head. "She raised a nice daughter."

"I raised myself. The credit belongs to me and me alone."

"What about your father?"

"I didn't know I had one until recently. I've found him, but I'm just working up the nerve to tell him."

"I'd be glad to help, Corinne."

"I'll think about it, okay? Good night."

Kani lay there for a while thinking about Corinne, grateful for the distraction. But not much time passed before Iain invaded her thoughts again. She filled the bathtub and soaked for a while, hoping the heat would help her sleep. As if in a trance, she brushed her hair until it crackled, then donned a silk robe over her naked body and left the room, committed to the life-altering decision she'd finally made.

Softly she padded down the stairs; quietly she moved down the hall; soundlessly she opened the door to Iain's room, closing it just as silently.

Iain watched her lean against the door, letting her eyes adjust to the darkness, or making up her mind, he didn't know which. Her fragrance assailed him, lemon and Kani. She took a few hesitant steps until she stood beside the bed, and he lifted the sheet in invitation, startling a gasp out of her.

Instantly she shrugged the robe off her shoulders and slid in beside him, into his open arms, into his loving embrace. Safe. Warm. *Home.*

"I don't care how much I get hurt," she said, her lips against his neck, her arms squeezing him as his hand made long, sweeping, tantalizing strokes down her back.

"You care."

"No."

"Maybe not tonight. But tomorrow. Or next week. Or next month."

"I've made my decision. You can't change it."

"You think I want to?" he asked harshly, bringing her solidly against him. He pushed her hand down to feel the magnitude of his desire, leaving no doubt as to how much he wanted her.

"You're already wearing—"

"I heard the bath and I knew it was you, imagined you lying naked in the tub. I knew you'd come. Is that egotistical? I don't think so. I just know you. I just damn know you. I want you, Kani. Like nothing I've ever wanted before. Having you in Mexico should have been enough—it wasn't. I've been dying staying away from you. All I've wanted is to touch, to stroke, to taste. All I've wanted is to have you moving against me, your eyes glazed with passion, your breasts crushed to my chest, your legs wrapped around mine, the pattern of your breathing shifting to soft moans of pleasure. Do you think for one minute I'd forgotten? Not for a minute, not for a second. Not even for a breath." He bent to her hungrily, kissed her deeply, longingly, impatiently, then lifted his head. "Tell me how you want it. Fast? Slow? Tell me."

"Fast," she whispered, mesmerized by the strength of him, by the command in his voice. "No. Slow. *I don't know.* I only know I don't need any foreplay beyond the words you just gave me."

He controlled every muscle in his body, curbing his almost violent need. "How about if we start fast...." He slipped into her as he spoke, his breath hot against her face, his gaze locked with hers. "Then we take it slow."

Kani arched in response, sucking in a deep breath as he filled her with himself, with his passion, with whatever emotions he was harboring. But she'd waited too long, remembered too well, loved too hard. So had Iain. Fulfillment came instantly, completely, staggeringly.

He sank against her, felt the hot wetness of tears rolling down her face and kissed them away, soothing her with wordless sounds, crushing her to him. After a long time, he moved off her, keeping her tucked tightly against him but settling them both more comfortably.

Peace. God, Kani, you bring such peace, he thought as he squeezed his eyes shut and combed her hair over and over with his fingers.

"I'll be here every night. You can't keep me away," she said.

"I won't try."

Kani awakened sore and content after the long night of lovemaking. Iain slept soundly beside her, and she smiled at his scruffy day-old beard and tangled hair. She lifted her hand to brush the hair out of his face and heard Gypsy meow at the door. That's what woke me up, she thought, finally registering the sound. She'd started to fold back the sheet to climb out of the bed when the door opened.

"Quiet, cat. I'm letting you in with him," she heard Corinne whisper to Gypsy, who flew through the opening just as Kani yanked the sheet up beneath her chin.

Her gaze met Corinne's and she watched the girl take in the scene before her. Kani felt her shock, her disapproval, then, ultimately, her devastation.

"Oh, my God," Kani said aloud as Corinne ran off and Iain stirred. "How could we have forgotten Corinne?"

"What's going on?" Iain asked. "Where are you going?"

"Corinne just saw us. I've got to go after her. Explain."

Iain grabbed her wrist. "No. It's just as well. This should kill the infatuation."

"Obviously you know nothing about impressionable young girls in love. You can't just ignore the situation, Iain. It won't disappear. But she might run away again. I don't want that on my conscience. Do you?"

He loosened his grip, and she swept up her robe before flying from the room, taking two stairs at a time and barging unannounced into Corinne's room. Her head was buried in her pillow and she was crying her heart out. Kani sat on the bed and placed a hand on her back. Corinne jerked violently away.

"He said you weren't involved," she said bitterly. "Liar. You're both liars."

"I'm sorry we hurt you. But, Corinne, Iain isn't interested in you that way. He's a grown man. He's too old for you."

Corinne sat up quickly. Her eyes were bright with tears she swiped at with the sleeve of her nightshirt. "You think I'm in *love* with him?"

"Aren't you?"

"No." Her voice held conviction and amazement. "You're wrong. I'm not in love with Iain. But I do love him. I've loved him since the first moment I saw him—when I was seven years old."

Twelve

"Seven ... years ... old?"

"Iain's my brother."

Stunned was too mild a word for what Kani felt. Staggered, astounded—those were closer in definition but still not enough. "I think you'd better explain," she said at last.

"We have the same mother. I thought we had different fathers, but now I know that's not true. We have the same father, as well."

"Please, Corinne. Start at the beginning." When she hesitated, Kani pushed. "I brought you into my home. I've trusted you when no one else did. *Trust* me, Corinne."

Corinne's mouth twisted as she considered Kani's words, then she tucked her knees under her chin. "I'll tell you what I've figured out so far. My mother left our father when Iain was a little boy. She moved to New York and started a successful career there. Obviously I don't know a lot about the circumstances surrounding my birth. She never talked about my father. I stopped asking because it seemed to upset her so much. During the school year, I lived in our house in

Connecticut with a couple who raised me as well as took care of the house and grounds. I was allowed to visit Mother in her penthouse in the city on an occasional weekend and during the summer.''

At the words ''I was allowed'' Kani's stomach contracted. The loneliness in the girl's voice filled the quiet room.

''I was seven when Iain arrived unannounced at the penthouse,'' Corinne continued. ''He must have been about twenty-two. I'd been drawing with my crayons in a little fort I'd made in the living room when he got there, so I just stayed hidden. I heard them talking and I could see him, but he couldn't see me. He had just found out that she wasn't dead, as his father had always told him. He demanded to know why she'd left, why she hadn't tried to contact him. He seemed to want to blame his father for everything. I guess his . . . *our* dad wasn't the greatest. But Mother was so cold to him—ice cold. It gave me chills.'' She shivered, then took a minute to let her memories come back again.

''I don't know why I didn't come out of hiding. I was afraid, I guess. But as much as Iain's anger intimidated me, I looked at him and saw the big brother I'd fantasized having, and I wanted to hug him. He didn't stay long. He was angry, really, really angry when he left. I came out of my fort and asked her why she'd left him. She was furious that I'd seen them together and heard what they'd talked about. I asked her about my father for the first time in years. She said the subject was closed, that my father had never wanted me. We were never to speak of him again.''

''You left it at that?'' Kani asked.

''I was seven years old! No, we never spoke of him again. But I dreamed about Iain—vivid dreams, fantasy dreams of a life that could have been, if only we'd had the chance to support each other. He'd been hurt. I'd been hurt. I thought if we were together it would be okay.''

''So how did you find him?''

''Early this summer I searched through my mother's papers while she was out of town. I didn't know Iain's last name. I had assumed he was the product of an earlier marriage. Then I found papers indicating Iain's last name, MacKenzie.''

"What name do you use?" Kani asked.

"My mother's professional name, which is not Mac-Kenzie. But what surprised me most was finding my own birth certificate. It listed a Darnell MacKenzie as my father. So I hired a private investigator to find Iain.''

"How could you afford that?''

Corinne's smile was bitter. "My mother wasn't generous with herself, but she was overly generous with money. I'd saved a lot, more than enough for my needs, more than enough to find my brother. But when I got to Los Angeles, he'd gone. The investigator tracked down Iain's agent and found out he'd moved up here. So I followed.''

"This is incredible,'' Kani said. "Why haven't you told Iain?''

"I wanted him to like me. I thought he'd go away if I told him who I was, that just because we had the same mother, he'd think I was like her. And I'm not.''

"Why haven't you contacted your father?''

"I don't know how he'd feel about meeting me. I don't even know if my parents are divorced. I wanted to talk to Iain first, to know what to expect when I met him. I didn't want to do it alone. He's my brother. He's supposed to help me.''

"I envy you and Bryan," Iain had said. Yes, he would adjust to having a sister well enough. Maybe. "When were you planning on telling him?''

"Right after the play opens. I figured the pressure would be off after that. Promise me you'll keep my secret until then.''

"Corinne— That is your real name, isn't it?''

"Yes.''

"I hate keeping this from him. He's been hurt a lot by women in his life, although I don't know all the details. Hearing your story makes me understand some of his pain. I wish you'd tell him now. The play's in good shape. He no longer needs to concentrate on it. And secrets like this always backfire.''

"Next week. I promise.''

Kani hesitated. "Why were you so upset to see us together this morning?''

"It's nothing against you personally. I want him free to spend time with me so that we can get to know each other, become a real brother and sister. If he's hung up on you, that won't happen.''

"I would never stand in the way of your getting to know each other. My brother Bryan's one of the most important people in my life. I'd never deny you the same chance to have Iain mean as much to you.'' Kani closed her eyes briefly. "I'll give you this week, and only this week, to continue your secret. But if you don't tell him next Saturday, I will. I won't risk my relationship with him over your secret. All right?''

"Thank you. I promise. Next Saturday.''

Kani moved quietly downstairs; she closed Iain's bedroom door behind her. He sat on the bed with Gypsy curled in the nest made by his crossed legs.

"Is she okay?'' he asked.

"She understands. And she's promised not to run away.''

"It really is for the best, Average.''

"I guess. Iain?''

"Hmm?''

She untied the sash of her robe and allowed the silk to whisper to a puddle at her feet. "Let's skip the gym this morning.''

Kani glanced up as Bryan stood framed in her bedroom doorway.

"I'm taking off for a few days,'' he said.

She debated silently a moment, then said, "I need to talk to you.''

"Come talk while I pack.''

"Meaning you'd like me to fold your clothes for you,'' she said, following him down the hall.

He turned to grin at her. "Well, as long as you're offer-
ng." A bag just large enough to stow under an airplane seat
ay open on his bed, a small stack of clothes beside it.

"I can never get over how light you travel." She rolled
lothes into tight tubes to discourage wrinkles, and Bryan
dded toiletries and a paperback novel for the flight.

"You seem happy," he said when she didn't seem in-
lined to start the conversation.

"I am happy."

"But you're guarding yourself against pain."

"I'm trying to, but I can't remember to do it for long. I
et swept up with the emotions and forget the eventuali-
ies."

"He cares a great deal for you."

"I know. In his own way, he cares. But I want a lifetime
ommitment, and he can't seem to let himself offer one."

Bryan sat beside her. "I'll tell you something he said to
ne, so that maybe you can understand him better. He asked
ne if, as a man, I could let myself fall for a woman who de-
erves the sun and the moon and the stars, if all I could give
er was a look through a telescope."

A bleak desperation filled Kani. "He doesn't even un-
lerstand me enough to know that I'd settle for just being
eld in his arms and *looking* at the sky with him."

"He understands. Deep down, he does. He's just very,
ery cautious."

"Like you."

He lifted a brow. "I'm not afraid of commitment. I just
an't offer it right now."

"How long will you continue? Until you're too old to
start a family—or you're dead?"

"Why the concern all of a sudden? You've always accepted what I do."

"No, I haven't. I just haven't pestered you about it."

"I'm rarely in danger, sis."

She put her arms around him and pressed her face against
his neck. "My whole future may rest on what happens during this week, and you're not going to be here. But I want

you to know how much I've loved being your sister. How
much I appreciate you. How much I value you."

"Hey, what's this? You think I'm going to die on you?"

She let go of him to wipe her eyes. "I'm just grateful to
have had you to count on all my life. You've been the best
brother a girl could hope for."

"And I'll continue to be." He cocked his head at her.
"You want to share what you think is going to happen this
week?"

"I can't. It isn't my secret to share. But wherever you are
Saturday night, please call me if you can. I'll tell you then."

"I'll try to be back by then, if it's so important."

"It's just inevitable, Bryan. We can't do anything about
it except wait and watch, and perhaps be allowed to pick up
the pieces."

"You know, I could delay this trip—"

"Go. It won't change anything."

Bryan sat in silence for a minute. "Is Mom flying up to
see the play?"

"Not until closing weekend."

"Have you told her about Iain?"

Kani chuckled. "A little."

"What's so funny?"

"You know Mom. She didn't ask me what he looks like,
or what he does for a living, or how we met. She asked if
Gypsy likes him."

"Huh?"

"She said that you could tell how good a father a man
would make by the way he treats his cat. Gypsy gives him a
thumbs-up."

For the first time since Ramshackle Theater had opened,
Kani was free to just watch and enjoy the play. For all the
countless other productions during her seven-year history
with it, she'd been either a performer or part of the backstage crew. This time she treated herself as an honored guest.

So many people had contributed to the effort. Wes with
his many contacts in the media, Julia with her beautiful

over art for the playbill, other old theater friends who had
volunteered to run lights and sound, handle props, run the
box office.

And the audience invited to attend the final dress rehearsal responded with tears and laughter. Kani's pride in
what they had accomplished together sent her soaring on an
incredible high. Nothing could go wrong this night. Nothing. The critics would come tomorrow; let them say what
they might. This was Kani's night.

After the dress rehearsal, she was too wound up to watch
"A Time to Love," so she took a hot bath instead, leaving
Corinne and Iain to tell her what had happened. She joined
them for the last five minutes.

"This is getting interesting," Corinne said to Kani.
"Carlotta told Daniel it's over."

"Finally," Kani replied. "They've made some good
changes recently. Funny how they seem to almost hear us,
isn't it?"

Corinne's gaze flickered toward Iain briefly, very briefly.
"Yeah. Funny. Well, big day tomorrow. I'm off to bed."
She smiled at them, turned off the light, and closed the door
behind her.

"I wonder what's gotten into her this week," Iain said.
"It's as if she underwent a personality transplant."

"She's been quiet, all right."

"You don't know the half of it. Usually she pesters me off
and on all day. This week she's left me completely alone."

Kani smiled as she wriggled her shoulders into her pillows. "Missed her, did you?"

"No. Well, sort of. I found I couldn't concentrate with all
that quiet. I guess she's grown on me, especially now that
her infatuation's been killed."

"She's a wonderful girl. You have to admit she's been
entertaining."

"I'll grant her that." He ran a hand down Kani's arm. "I
think I'll take a quick shower. Meet you downstairs in a few
minutes?"

"Perfumed and waiting."

He nuzzled her neck. "You don't need to add perfume fo me. I like the way your skin smells of just you and soap."

"Go. Hurry," she urged, instantly aroused.

Ten minutes later, he emerged from the adjoining bath room into a pitch-black bedroom. "Why'd you shut th blinds?" he asked. "I can barely see you."

"Exactly."

"But I like to watch you," he said softly as he move closer. "Watch the look on your face, watch the way yo arch into me, the way we fit together. Watch—" He sud denly stopped talking as he peeled the sheet back.

Her body was alive with light. "What in the world—?" he said in amazement.

Kani looked down at herself. She was dotted with glow-in the-dark stickers. "Oh my goodness! How did that hap pen?"

"Where did you... How did... Kani?"

"They weren't there earlier. You... you must have give them to me."

"I... I gave you...?"

"The sun and the moon and the stars. How odd. I hadn' even asked for them, but here they are. Did you wish them for me, Iain?"

Touched almost beyond speech, he trailed his fingertip along the glowing celestial beings serpentining down he body. "I must have. I wanted so much to give them to you."

"And so you have."

His tongue swept circles along the edges of the stickers following one to another as if it were a dot-to-dot puzzle connecting a pattern of passion, a design of desire. He drev her over him, reveling in the feel of her skin gliding over hi as he settled her on him.

"Don't move," he whispered.

She kept still as he molded her breasts in his hands, traile the taut skin of her abdomen, and pressed a thumb to th center of her desire. He loved the way her head droppe back and her body arched.

"You're so damned perfect," he said, almost cursing the ct. "My own heavenly body."

Kani leaned over him, her hair falling like a curtain ound her face. "I love you, Iain."

"Kani." The word rasped against his raw throat. "Kani."

"You don't have to say anything. I just couldn't hold it any longer. Make love to me, Iain. Hold me. Kiss me."

"I'll hold you. Cherish you. And by God, I'll love you. I love you. *I . . . love . . . you.*"

He affirmed his confession with tender caresses and end-ss kisses that built into a need so strong they heard noth-g but sighs and moans, felt nothing but each other's easure, delaying that final ecstasy again and again, owing each other so well they knew the exact moment to come motionless, to let the climb to the pinnacle slip a tch, then start anew. *Oh, yes, there. Like that. More. Oh, ore. Wait. Don't move. Oh! Again. Please, again. I love e way you taste. I love the way you touch me. I love you!*

And he never once opened the drawer of his bedside ta-e. She'd won his trust at last.

Kani's laughter echoed in the bathroom. Her stickers, ch a flight of fancy, also proved to be painful to remove. e'd been soaking in a hot tub for half an hour. Finally, e by one, the stickers were floating to the top, where Iain ught them with a fingertip and spread them on the vanity dry, announcing his intent to keep them as mementos.

She watched the tender way he handled the bits of paper d knew his emotions were stretched taut. There had been most more emotion than she could handle, so she figured must be painfully aware of his own feelings right now. e closed her eyes and smiled. He trusted her. Now all she d to do was get him to see that marriage and fatherhood ould be wonderful, too. He was a tough sell, cautious at ery step of their relationship, and taking a long time to get mfortable with each new emotion. They cared deeply out each other, though, and that should be enough to ld them until he finally came around.

"Why the secretive little smile?" he asked as he caught a quarter moon and laid it on the tile vanity.

She opened her eyes. "Do I look secretive? I'm just happy."

"Maybe secretive is the wrong word. You look...satisfied."

Her smile widened. "I am."

"I don't mean sexually."

Kani watched him avoid her gaze. He'd told her once that words were easy, but she could see he was having trouble putting into words what he felt. "What *do* you mean?"

He shrugged. "Pleased with yourself, I guess."

She sat up; the movement dislodged the last few stars, and they bobbed over the waves she created when she moved. "I am pleased with *you*. Are you regretting your words?"

"No. No." He spread out the last few stars, then dried his hands on his thighs. "I'm just not comfortable talking about my feelings."

"I'm not complaining, Iain. Tell me what you want to when you want to. I won't push you."

"I appreciate that about you, you know. You don't question me. You don't ask for more than I can give."

"I figure you'll share when you want to."

"Bartender's training?"

She shook her head slowly. "Vice versa, I think. I'm successful in my job because I have the right personality for it."

"You don't pass judgment."

"I try not to. But I'm human. I react, sometimes too quickly or too vigorously. I've given up on you several times, then found hope again the next day."

He loosened the knot of hair on her head and let the gold shot dark tresses fall around her shoulders and cling to her wet skin. "Obviously Bryan shared a discussion we had about you, hence the stickers."

"And you're wondering what else he told me?" At his nod, she placed her hand against the side of his face and turned him toward her. "Nothing. He confided nothing beyond the fact you thought I deserved the sun and the moon and the stars, but that you couldn't give them to me. He keeps confidences, Iain. Whatever other secrets he holds are safe."

"He's tougher than most fathers grilling a daughter's date."

"So I've heard. He's a good brother. A good man."

"Yes." He brushed her cheek with his knuckles. "I love you."

"Feels good to say it, doesn't it?"

Iain nodded his head, then pulled her against him, splattering water over the tub and onto the floor. "It feels good, period. You feel good. Let's turn this evening into a memory. Let's not forget any of it. Let's tell each other how we feel every step of the way, and we'll repeat it and memorize it all."

"I never realized you were such a romantic."

He lifted her chin, then kissed her, a slow, flaming tease that touched, retreated, touched again, then settled and intensified before he lifted his head and pressed his lips to her forehead. "Neither did I."

Thirteen

―

"Kani, we need you at the box office."

She groaned into the backstage intercom. "I'm not supposed to do anything, Louise. I'm supposed to be a guest tonight."

"Guest or not, lady, you're still the boss, and we've got a problem only you can handle."

"Can't you just tell me what it is?"

"W-e-l-l, I *could*. But I think you need to see this to believe it."

Intrigued now, Kani grinned. "I'll be right there."

She exited through a side door into the theater and wove her way past the patrons standing and talking in the aisles during the ten minutes before curtain. She shook her head in wonder. Her tiny little theater was populated with sequined ladies and tuxedoed gentlemen, like an opening night at the opera. Generally the most fashionable of her patrons wore sport coats or simple work dresses. Until this gala evening, no one had ever dressed up for Ramshackle. Kani had rented a dress for the evening, a ruby red sequined, an-e-length, one-shouldered sheath that molded her curves d undulated with each step she took. Her hair was fashned into an elegant twist and studded with faux ruby irpins. She felt sophisticated, beautiful even. Iain had en speechless.

Kani ducked through a door into the office and headed r the ticket counter. Louise stopped her before she could ss into public view.

"A customer showed up without a reservation," she said.

Kani's brows lifted. "We're sold-out. Unless someone esn't show up in the last couple of minutes, they'll have come back another time. You know all this, Louise. Why e you bothering me with it?"

"Take a look through the door and see who you're tellg to wait."

Kani inched around Louise and spotted a tall, slender, lver-haired woman gowned in black silk and wrapped in a lver fox fur that Kani hoped was just an excellent imitaon. The woman turned toward Kani.

"Oh, my! It's Helena Hunt."

"You got it," Louise said. "Now what?"

"What's she doing here?"

"That's not exactly something I thought I should ask, ani. She's adamant about seeing the play."

"Good grief, why? Well, I guess she can have my seat. I'll t in the light booth." She grinned. "Robert and Iain can ntertain her. I wonder how she heard about this play? I lought she rarely left New York. She's starring in something on Broadway right now, isn't she?"

"Park Place."

"That's right. So what's she doing here? Oh, well. I'll ke care of her. Thanks, Lou."

Kani made a quick exit out of the office and hurried into le waiting area. People were staring at and whispering bout the actress, who was one of the few New York theter performers recognizable anywhere by anyone.

"Miss Hunt, I'm Kani Warner, owner of the Ramhackle. Welcome to our theater."

The great lady looked Kani up and down.

"I'll be happy to show you to your seat."

"I hope it's good."

"Between the director and the playwright. Is that sui[t]-able?" Lord, spare me from egotistical, demanding pe[r]-formers, Kani thought. She focused on Iain already sitti[ng] in his seat, too nervous to do anything but roll his progra[m] tighter and tighter. He turned his head and smiled as s[he] neared, obviously glad to see her. Then he saw the woma[n] behind her and his face blanched. Kani almost laughed [at] his expression. We all get a little star struck, she though[t], even the Iains of the world.

"Iain," Kani began, "Miss Hunt will be sitting next [to] you."

Iain stood, stiff and controlled. "What the hell are y[ou] doing here?" he asked the actress.

Bewildered, Kani looked from Iain to Helena. "Y[ou] know each other?"

"No," Iain replied before turning his back on them an[d] walking away.

"Iain," she said, beseeching him with an outstretch[ed] hand. Suddenly aware of the murmuring around them, Ka[ni] quickly introduced Helena to Robert, then went after Iai[n].

Gone. He was gone. Louise said she hadn't noticed hi[m] pass by. Maybe he was in the rest room. What was going o[n]? And how did he know Helena Hunt, unless—

A horrible suspicion flashed into her mind. *Unless s[he] was his mother*. It made sense. If his play truly was autob[i]-ographical, his mother had left his father to go to New Yor[k] to become an actress. And what about Corinne? Lord, wh[at] was she going to do? It was all going to come to a head t[o]-night in turmoil instead of tomorrow in relative peace an[d] quiet. Should she warn Corinne? Find Iain? Could she leav[e] the theater?

"We're ready to start, Kani," Louise said.

"What? Oh, fine. Alert the booth, will you? I've got t[o] go outside for a minute."

His car was gone. At least one question was answered. Now what to do? *Trust him.* The words reverberated in her mind. Trust him not to run away. Trust him to be at home waiting. Go back into the theater and do what you have to do. Overwhelmingly sad that Iain was missing this big moment in his life, Kani made her way into the light booth to watch the play.

Putting together what Iain had revealed little by little to Kani with what Corinne had shared made Kani believe the play was almost completely autobiographical. She watched *Journeys* as if for the first time, watched six-year-old Johnny—Iain?—stand before his father like a miniature soldier as he was told his mother was dead. The eight-year-old actor playing Johnny portrayed the devastated child brilliantly, his mouth quivering, as his father ordered him to buck up. "Men don't cry," the father said harshly. The child walked on shaking legs to his bedroom, burying his face in a pillow and crying, the eerie, unearthly, almost animal-like wail affecting even the most hard-bitten observers.

The scene shifted to Johnny—now insisting he be called John—at age sixteen, fending off an attempt by his father's girlfriend to seduce him. Then the eighteen-year-old was graduating from high school and leaving his father's home the same day. There was a shift to the revelation that his mother was alive and his attempt to find her—and his futile attempt to discover why she'd abandoned him. She'd revealed nothing to him, forcing him to come to terms with her desertion without solid reasons, only his own painful speculation.

Kani felt a depth of compassion such as she'd never known—for the small, bewildered boy, for the lanky, confused teenager, for the child in a man's shell who struggled to understand. Her gaze returned again and again to Helena Hunt. Iain's mother. Corinne's mother.

More than anything, Kani just wanted to go home and hold him—rock the boy, hug the teenager, make love to the man.

I'm coming, Iain. Don't leave. I'm coming.

"Is Helena Hunt your mother?" Kani asked Corinne harshly as soon as she could get backstage after the play.

"How did you know?"

"She's here. In the audience."

"Oh, my God! What's she *doing* here? Did Iain see her? She's going to ruin everything."

"Iain saw her and turned his back on her. He left. Go home, Corinne. Hope and pray that Iain is there, and tell him the truth right now. You can't delay another second."

"What about you? He'll need you."

"I can't leave yet."

"I can't, Kani. I can't talk to him alone."

"He's your brother, for God's sake. And he's not a stranger to you. You've been living in the same house for weeks."

"Please, I can't tell him myself. I'll wait for you."

The girl was wringing her hands; Kani relented. "All right. I'll find someone to drive us home. Do you think your mother is here because of Iain or you?"

"I don't know. Iain, I guess. How would she know I was here?"

"I thought maybe you'd finally called her."

"No. I figured I would tomorrow, after I told...Iain...the truth." Her eyes were bleak. "I waited too long, didn't I?"

"Looks like it. We'll do the best we can. Do you want to see your mother?"

"No!"

Kani placed a comforting hand on Corinne's arm. "I'll call you on the intercom when I'm ready to go. Will you be all right?"

"I guess. I'll start rehearsing what to say to Iain."

"Good. Relax. Maybe it won't be as bad as you think."

"Sure."

Kani's mouth curved into a grim smile as she left.

"Miss." The voice was haughty, distinct and commanding.

"Yes, Miss Hunt?"

"The playwright, where could I find him to congratulate im?"

"He left the theater, ma'am."

"Oh, that's too bad. Would you mind passing along a iessage?"

"Not at all."

"Please tell him if he's interested in bringing his play to Jew York, I'd be happy to help."

"Why?" The word was said politely enough, but Kani's heer audacity at questioning the older woman obviously urprised Helena.

"It's a good play. A good role for a woman my age. They're getting harder and harder to come by."

"You'd be willing to play the mother's role? After all the ig roles you've had?"

"This one is...special. A character with depth, and laws."

"Yes, she definitely has flaws," Kani said, showing nei- her sympathy nor understanding for the cold, haughty voman standing before her. She had abandoned Iain. She ad all but abandoned Corinne. Kani couldn't forgive her or that. "I'm glad you came tonight, Miss Hunt. I hope ou enjoyed it. Now, if you'll excuse me, I have business to ttend to."

"Of course, my dear. Please call me a cab so that I may eturn to my hotel."

Kani inclined her head and walked rigidly into her office. She leaned against the door after she closed it and pressed her forehead against the cold metal. Every time life seemed to settle down, a tornado whirled through it, knocking the foundation out from under her. One problem solved, an- other one born. She sank into her desk chair and dialed the phone to request a taxi. After cradling the receiver, she took three deep breaths, smoothed the frown from her forehead, and left her temporary haven.

When the theater was empty, Kani and Corinne hitched a ride home from a cast member.

"Wait in the living room," Kani said to Corinne as the climbed the steps to the house. "If he's in his room, I'll tal to him first."

"Okay. Oh, I'm so nervous."

"Me, too."

Kani could see light at the bottom of Iain's bedroom door She knocked. "Iain?"

A brief silence. "Come in."

The click of the latch seemed extraordinarily loud t Kani; the hinges squeaked. He lay on the bed, clad in jean and T-shirt, staring at the ceiling. "The play was a big suc cess," she said.

"Great."

"Robert thinks the reviews will be outstanding."

"Terrific." His voice lacked any inflection whatsoever Flat words uttered without emotion.

She sat beside him and cupped his arm in her hand "Want to talk?"

He closed his eyes. "Helena Hunt is my mother."

"Yes, I figured that out."

"Why was she there, Kani? She hasn't paid a bit of at tention to me for twenty-six years. I've seen her only onc in all that time, and that was for less than ten minutes."

"I don't know. The play got so much attention in th media that word of it probably reached New York."

"Why would that bring her here? She's never cared abou me. Why the sudden maternal interest?"

Kani rubbed his cold skin. "She told me to tell you tha she would help you bring the play to New York if yo wanted. She seemed interested in playing what I assume i herself."

Iain laughed without humor. "I see. She was just scout ing out a new role. Things must be getting tough for her now that she's past her prime. She'll never act in my play, tha much I can tell you. I hate her. God, I hate her. She jus about destroyed my life, Kani. For your mother not to love you . . . do you have any idea how much that hurts? Wha could I have done as a child to make her leave me?"

Kani swallowed. "I don't think it was you. I think it was her. She needed something different in her life. Maybe your father forced her to choose. And maybe she made the wrong choice, but the only choice for her."

"Are you defending her?"

"No, never. I'm trying to understand, too."

"There's no excuse, Kani. None."

"I think there's always an excuse, or a reason, for the things we do. We all do things we regret."

"Decent people regret. Helena Hunt is not a decent person."

She brushed the hair away from his forehead; his skin was clammy. "I hate to add to your burdens tonight, but I need you to come to the living room with me."

He turned his gaze sharply on her.

"It's not Helena," she said quickly, interpreting his expression. "It's something else. Please come."

He sat up, then prevented her from standing by cupping her face with his hand. "I haven't talked about my mother to anyone for ten years."

She pressed her lips briefly to his, sending her warmth, transferring her strength, telegraphing her love. *Be strong, Iain. Be understanding. Corinne needs you and you need her.*

"Corinne?" Iain asked in surprise when he entered the living room and saw the teenager. He looked around the room for another person and turned to Kani. "What's going on?"

Corinne squeezed her hands together. "I have something to tell you—"

The doorbell rang. Kani and Corinne exchanged panicked looks. Had Helena tracked down Iain? Her nerves already in tatters, Corinne burst into tears and ran from the room.

"What the hell?" Iain said in confusion as he watched Corinne run off and Kani move to the front door.

"You!" a haughty voice announced. "Warner. Of course I should have guessed. Well, where is she? Where's my daughter?"

Helena pushed Kani aside and came face-to-face with Iain. "Ah. So you know about her, do you? I should have figured she'd track you down."

"Who? Who are you talking about?" Iain asked.

"Your sister, of course."

"My...sister...?" Understanding dawned on his face. "Corinne is my sister." Not a question; a statement of fact. A cold, hard, angry statement of fact.

"You didn't know?"

Iain was breathing heavily. "Corinne! Get out here," he yelled toward the kitchen. "Right now!"

Corinne quaked visibly as she returned to the living room. Kani stood in silence, wanting to let Iain lean on her, wanting to hold Corinne, as well. One woman shouldn't have so much power over someone's emotions, Kani thought angrily.

Corinne ventured a look at Iain. "I was...going to tell you...tomorrow...after the play...." Her voice faded with each word, and she turned her head away.

Iain grabbed her arm and swung her around to face him. He studied her face for truths. Disgusted, he shoved her toward Helena.

"Well, darling, you've really done it this time, haven't you," Helena said to Corinne, who jerked away from her mother's touch. "If I'd had any idea you were with Iain, I would have come much sooner. If he's anything like his father—"

"I'm not. *I* feel," Iain snarled. "If my *sister* is anything like you—"

"I'm not!" Corinne put herself toe-to-toe with him. "*I* feel, too. More than you can imagine. I've dreamed of us being a real family for a very long time."

"What? How could you? And obviously you're my *half* sister."

"No, I'm not. My father is Darnell MacKenzie. Is that our father?"

Iain's head snapped back. Staggered, his knees went weak. "How old are you?"

"Seventeen."

"But my parents were divorced when I was—" He turned to Helena. "Weren't you?"

"No."

Iain shook his head. "I don't understand this. I don't understand any of this."

"Your father and I never divorced. Neither of us cared to. Believe it or not, we've never stopped loving each other."

"Right," Iain said with a disbelieving snort. "You're the epitome of American family values, aren't you? *I thought you were dead.* I wasn't even allowed to ask questions about you. Your name never came up until I was twenty-two and needed my birth certificate to apply for a passport. For the heck of it, I had an investigator look into your background, just so I'd know something about you. You were alive and well, the toast of Broadway, living in a penthouse overlooking Central Park. I'd grown up in a crumbling apartment in Hollywood." He looked at Corinne. "Our lives couldn't have been more different."

"Maybe not so different, Iain. I rarely saw Mother. Most of the year I lived in Connecticut, where I wouldn't interfere with her social life. She kept me a secret, you know. You didn't have love and attention? Well, neither did I. I just lived in better surroundings."

"Why didn't you tell me?"

"As I told Kani, I wanted you to like me—"

"You knew?" Iain turned on Kani. "You knew she was my sister and you didn't tell me?"

"I just found out a week ago—"

Iain dragged her close to him. "I trusted you."

"It wasn't my secret to tell, Iain."

"Please, Iain. Don't blame her," Corinne beseeched him. "I begged her to let me be the one."

"A week. You've known a week." He looked at the three women, each so different. And each so alike to him. He pulled Kani away from the others. "I have to leave."

"No—"

He grasped her arms with both hands, and their gazes locked. "I can't deal with this right now. I've got to go home and sort it out."

"Oh, Iain. I understand how overwhelming this all must be to you. But to go away...?"

"I'm not like you, Kani. I don't talk things through. I have to think them through."

She threw herself against him, squeezing tightly. Then she let him go, watching with stoic acceptance as he turned away from the love and understanding she offered.

"You can't!" Corinne cried, running after him. "I just found you! I've waited ten years to find you, and I'm not letting go of you now. I want a brother! I need a brother! *My* brother! Please, Iain. Don't push me away. We can help each other."

Iain shook off her hands. "We'll talk. But not now. Not yet."

He left. Helena stood straight and still. Corinne cried loud and hard. Kani died a little.

Minutes later, when the last sounds of the car engine faded into the night, each woman reacted differently. Helena sighed and lightly brushed the elegant fur covering her arms. Corinne sobbed quietly. Kani sank into a chair and buried her face against Gypsy's warm body after she jumped into her lap. Finally Kani lifted her head.

"Get out of my house," she said to Helena.

"It's my understanding this house is owned by Bryan Warner, who must be a relative of yours?"

"How do you know that?"

"He called me weeks ago to tell me Corinne was here, safe. He assured me she was being well taken care of—"

"Like that makes a difference to you," Corinne said with a sneer. "You never checked on me at home. Did you even know I'd been gone before Bryan called?"

"Well, I—"

"Ha! You see, Kani? She thought I was spending a month with friends in Cape Cod. She didn't even know I was missing. Some kind of mother, huh?"

"Pack your bags and come with me, young lady. Your adventure has ended."

"No."

"What did you say?"

"I said no. I'm going to follow Iain. He's going to accept me as his sister. And I'm never going to live with you, accept anything from you, or call you Mother ever again."

"You are a minor—"

"Only for a few more months."

"You'll need money."

"I've got enough money. And Iain will take care of me."

"Iain doesn't want anything to do with you."

"As soon as he figures out we've both been victims, he'll accept me. Maybe he won't trust me, thanks to you, but that doesn't mean he'll turn his back on me. You can leave now." Corinne punctuated her words with a slow exit up the stairs, leaving Kani alone with Helena.

"I don't know how you sleep nights," Kani said.

An unreadable expression crossed the woman's face. "Sometimes I don't," she whispered.

Kani thought she heard regret in the tone. But how could you tell with the world's greatest actress? "Maybe it isn't too late to make amends," Kani suggested.

"Oh, my dear. It's far too late. I set my course the day I left my son behind so that I could pursue my career."

"May I ask you a few questions?" Kani asked.

"Yes, I suppose."

"Why did Iain's father pretend you were dead?"

"We made a deal. I could go to New York, but Iain had to stay with him."

"Why? Hollywood isn't any more stable than New York. And why death? Why not the truth?"

"Those were Darnell's terms. I think he thought to frighten me into staying by forcing me to give up all claims

to my son, but my desire to star on Broadway was stronger
You needn't frown at me. I'm not saying my decision was a
good one. It was just the only one for me. Darnell had
steady work that he liked. Moving to New York mean
starting over. He didn't want to do that."

"But after you were established, why didn't he go to you
then so you could be a family? You said you've always loved
each other."

"I tried to talk him into it many, many times. We'd meet
every so often for a weekend or longer, make love, argue,
part in anger, then make arrangements to see each other
again in a few months. I got pregnant on purpose. I though
it would force him into bringing us together. Unfortunately
my plan backfired. He's never acknowledged Corinne because he doesn't believe she's his. I never took lovers in New
York until years after Corinne was born, years after Darnell had stopped meeting me for our secret rendezvous."

"Would you live with him now?"

"No. No, our lives have changed too much. Too much
has happened along the way. He'd never be happy in New
York, and I can't give up what I sacrificed so much for."

"Iain says his father is a cold man."

"Iain sees only one side of his father—the angry man.
The small-town boy who married his childhood sweetheart, ventured west, and had his heart broken. Darnell is
bitter. He has a right to be."

"He didn't have a right to take it out on Iain."

"We take out our anger on those closest to us."

"As you did with Corinne, when you punished her by removing her from your life. You created pawns for you and
Darnell to push around. What a cruel, unfeeling, unloving
thing to do to two innocent children. And the legacy you've
given them haunts them every day."

"Yes, I could see that in Iain's play. It was quite extraordinary, you know. I didn't understand how much I had hurt
him until tonight. I didn't understand what his life had been
like."

"Does knowing it now change anything?"

Helena's smile was sad. "I doubt it. But who knows? Maybe there's hope." She stood, pulled her coat more tightly around her, and drew back the curtain. "Good, the driver's still there. I paid him enough to keep him, but you never know."

Kani also stood. "What about Corinne?"

"I think I'll let her make her own decisions for now."

"What about school?"

"It won't hurt her to take a few weeks off. She's a good student. I'm sure she can catch up. Please, thank Mr. Warner for his kindness in letting me know where she was. Here's a card with my phone number and address. Please call if you need me."

"Will you respond?"

Helena winced. "I deserve that, I suppose. I know I've forfeited a lot, but I'm not as unfeeling as you imply. They are my flesh and blood. I do care."

Kani watched Helena climb into the cab, then she shut the front door and walked directly to Iain's bedroom. He had taken everything, must have jammed his clothes into his bags, he'd packed and gone so fast. A light coating of dust framed where his computer had sat on the desk. Drawers sagged open, empty. The closet door stood ajar; hangers tangled on the floor and were jammed into the doorway, obviously dropped in a hurry as clothes were stripped off them. The bed still held his imprint. She lifted the pillow to breathe his scent, hugging it to her, knowing she'd take it upstairs to embrace through the night.

For however many nights it took for him to come home.

Fourteen

Iain awoke when sunlight pierced his eyelids. Groaning, he covered his eyes with an arm, but the heat forced him to withdraw the human shade. It had been dark when he'd finally pulled into his garage; he hadn't thought to close the blinds in his bedroom. He hadn't thought, period.

God, what a night. Anger had kept his adrenaline flowing so that he hadn't even needed to stop for coffee the first three hours. Then a kind of post-trauma lethargy had settled in, and he had struggled to stay awake after that. A gallon of coffee and periodic walks in the brisk night air had kept him from falling asleep at the wheel.

His house had smelled stale, hot, dry. Empty. No plants, no pets, no Kani. No life. Things like this just didn't happen to him. He'd guarded against emotional involvement for so long, then suddenly his life had overflowed with emotion. And he had no idea how to handle it.

He had a sister. That was the biggest shock of all.

Kicking back the sheet, he stretched in the sun's rays, closed his eyes, and tried to forget the last twelve hours by bsorbing the heat and light into his emotionally drained ody. It worked for a minute or two, then reality filtered hrough the hedonistic pleasure of the moment. Unwilling o go through further self-examination, he rolled out of bed nd yanked on a pair of shorts. Stumbling down the hall, he vandered into the kitchen, and opened the refrigerator loor, a move born purely of habit since he knew there vouldn't be anything there.

He was wrong. There was a third of a bottle of catsup, wo light beers, an almost empty jar of grape jelly and an unopened can of black olives. With a deep sigh, he pulled out a beer and the olives and set them on the counter. Rummaging through drawers for his can opener gave him a moment to consider the possible effects of black olives and beer on an empty stomach. He tossed the two cans back into he refrigerator and decided on a shower instead.

He did a good job of ignoring the reason he was home until he wiped the steam off the mirror so that he could have. Digging the razor out of his shaving kit made him pause. He'd shaved Kani's legs with it . . . was it just yesterday morning? She'd been so afraid he'd nick her that he had taken forever to accomplish the small task, and they both had been amazed at what an erotic act it was.

Iain leaned against the edge of the sink, the razor dangling from his fingertips. Finally he flung the blade into the wastebasket, then slammed the edge of the sink with his hand, hard. He stood leaning over the sink, breathing erratically, forcing images away.

He thought he knew her, understood her. He had liked that he could usually predict her feelings before she shared them. He'd thought her complex but uncomplicated, if that made any sense. That she had withheld the knowledge of Corinne's relationship was stunning.

And honorable, he decided.

He loved her. Of that he had no doubt, no question, no hesitation. But he couldn't go back to her until he could offer her marriage, as well. He knew she wanted that, deserved that. As for children, that was another decision.

He gave up on shaving—he didn't want to look at him
self in the mirror—passed a comb quickly through his hai
brushed his teeth, then dug through the bags he'd stuffed hi
clothes into, finding a wrinkled but clean pair of shorts an
T-shirt. Slipping into sandals while jamming his wallet int
his pocket, he made a mental shopping list as a way to avoi
thinking.

The living room blinds were coated with dust that drifte
onto the sill as he tilted them open. Good. The place neede
a thorough cleaning, and he needed a mindless task. H
flung open the front door and almost tripped over the per
son who had been sitting against the door and who now fel
backward against him.

"What the—! What are you doing here?" He loome
over her.

Corinne grinned upside down at him. "Came to visit m
big brother."

Iain scowled. "You weren't invited."

"Sisters don't need invitations." She straightened an
stood, then brushed her seat off.

"Everyone needs an invitation, especially you, brat."

Her smile grew wider. "See? You used your pet name fo
me. You care."

"You're the only person on the face of this earth wh
would consider brat a pet name."

"It's not the word, big brother. It's the tone of voice. Ca
I come in?"

"No."

"Why not?"

"I'm going to the store."

"I won't rob you while you're gone."

"How'd you get here?" he asked abruptly.

"Airplane."

"I hope you've got enough money to get home."

Corinne clucked her tongue. "You're not being very so-
ciable, Iain."

"I have no reason to be. I need to be alone. I told you
that. Can't you understand that?"

"No."

He stepped past her and pulled the door shut. "Have a
ce life, Corinne."

He hardened his heart against her crestfallen expression,
rned his back on the tears welling in her eyes, and de-
ended the steps in record time. He wasn't ready for this,
asn't ready for a confrontation with his newfound rela-
ve, wasn't ready to care. First take care of Iain, he thought.
hen worry about everyone else.

But she was there when he got back. She didn't say a
ord, just followed his movements with her eyes as he went
and out of the condo carrying groceries. He forced him-
lf not to look at her as he shut the door.

Iain peeked through the blinds for the sixth time in as
any hours. Still there. Corinne sat in perfectly planned
ewing range midway on the stairs, her head resting against
e railing, her foot tapping in rhythm to the music coming
rough her Walkman. As far as he could tell, she hadn't
ten, hadn't left her post. Which meant she hadn't used a
st room in hours and hours.

He leaned against the wall beside the window, then moved
earily to the front door and opened it. Her head turned
stantly toward him.

"Come in," he said simply.

Corinne bounded up the stairs.

"Bathroom's that way," he said, pointing.

She smacked a quick kiss on his cheek, dropped her
ackpack on the nearest chair, then ran down the hall.
Vhen she emerged a few minutes later, she followed the
mell of spaghetti sauce into the kitchen. "Am I invited to
inner or just for the pit stop?"

"You can stay."

"Your enthusiasm is overwhelming, big brother."

"Don't call me that."

She raised her brows. "Why not? It's what you are." As
e continued to work in silence, she began searching cup-

boards and drawers so that she could set the table. "Rath«
Spartan life you live, *Iain.*"

"I've never needed much." He drained pasta into a co
ander, then dumped it into a bowl.

"Until Kani."

Iain fixed a fierce stare on her. "My relationship wit
Kani is not open for discussion."

"I don't see why you're blaming her. She—"

"You're treading on thin ice, kid. How I feel about Ka
and what I do about it are not your concern. Period. G«
it?"

"Okay, okay." She picked up the triangle of Parmesa
cheese and began grating it onto the cutting board. "Can v
talk about Mother?"

"Absolutely not." He ladled marinara sauce over th
pasta.

Corinne sighed. "If we can't talk about the things we hav
in common, what can we talk about?"

"Who needs to talk?"

"We have a lifetime to catch up on. I want to get to kno
you."

"We've spent almost two months together. We know eac
other pretty well."

She put the dish of grated cheese on the table and sa
down as he did. "Our relationship before now was ham
pered by your irritation with me. Now that you know I'r
not some teenager with a crush on you, we can really com
municate." She put a hand on his as he reached for th
cheese. "I love you, Iain. That's something I've never sai«
to anyone or heard from anyone."

Iain stared at the table. He'd been envious of Kani an«
Bryan. Now he had a chance to share the same special re
lationship with his own sister. He'd seen what it meant t«
trust another person completely, as Kani and Bryan did
These thoughts flashed through the turmoil in his mind in «
matter of seconds. Then suddenly he stood, jerked Corinn«
into his arms, and buried his face in her hair. They held eac
other, more than a few tears falling.

And because he'd learned to say the words just recently
nd found they weren't so hard to say, after all, he told his
•aby sister he loved her, too.

"He'll call. He'll be back." Half prayer, half vow, the
vords were ones Kani repeated to herself, her brother, Jake,
Ves and Julia; even Gypsy heard the litany day in and day
•ut. Iain loved her. He'd said so; he'd shown it in his gaze,
is touch, his tenderness. He'd laughed with her, soothed
er, indulged her, fought with her. He'll come to his senses;
e won't give up something so right, so perfect. He'd be a
ool—

Kani's gloved fist slammed against the punching bag with
a loud thud. *He is a fool.* And she was a fool for letting him
continue to haunt her. He'd been gone over two weeks—
ong, tortuous weeks. He hadn't seen his play performed
•efore a sold-out house, hadn't seen the glowing reviews,
aadn't accepted his accolades.

She attacked the bag with renewed vigor, alternately
hrowing a punch, then bouncing on the balls of her feet,
;tepping back, then delivering a punishing, satisfying blow
.o the inanimate object. Her grunts came in no rhythmic
pattern but were effective combatants against frustration
and depression. She knew Julia and Bryan watched her with
matching expressions of concern on their faces. Julia had
taken Iain's desertion personally, angry that she'd been
wrong in her judgment of him. She'd credited him with
more courage than he'd shown. Bryan was more circum-
spect, offering Kani comfort and a shoulder to cry on but
reserving criticism of Iain.

Bryan had pushed through his assignment to return home
on that Saturday, only to find the dust already settling. He'd
been stunned at the revelation that Iain and Corinne were
brother and sister, although he admitted to Kani he'd
thought it more than coincidental that the daughter of a
Broadway star would end up at a certain little theater in San
Francisco.

"Why didn't you ask her about it?" Kani had asked the day Bryan returned home.

"She was adjusting well, seemed content." He shrugged. "Her mother knew she was safe, and I thought if she caught wind her cover was blown, she'd run. Helena had agreed to wait until school was ready to start before coming for her. She must have heard about Iain's play and combined two trips into one."

"How did you know who Corinne was?"

"No great detective job. I waited until she got into the shower one morning, then I looked for ID in her backpack. Simple."

Corinne had packed and left by the time Bryan had arrived home. Kani had spent hours curled on Corinne's bed talking with her, cautioning her not to get her hopes up where Iain was concerned. Like a wounded animal, he needed time to lick his wounds. Corinne's attempt to insinuate herself into his life might backfire.

"And it might not," Corinne had said. "I can be just as stubborn as he is."

"What if he isn't at home? How will you live?"

"I'll find him through his job. They'll know where he is. Believe me, I've learned all the acting skills I need from my mo—from Helena. I can find him."

"What job? I thought he was working for Wes."

Corinne had cocked her head at Kani. "You're really dense sometimes, you know. Iain's a writer for 'A Time to Love.'"

"He would have said—"

"He worked here at home. I could hear him on the phone for hours at a time, and he'd be saying the names of the characters on the show."

"But I always read the credits. His name isn't there as a writer."

"John MacKenzie. John, the Anglo-Saxon version of Iain."

"John ... Yes. You're right. I do remember that name. But he told me he'd been fired."

"I don't know the details. I only know that's what he did
hile you were at work. That and some work for Wes. He
rely left his room all day."

So now even her nighttime tranquilizer was gone. Kani
opped watching the soap, stopped taping it. Stopped car-
g. Too much had been happening on the show that she
alized had come from conversations they'd had, either just
e two of them, or with Julia and Corinne. And she
uldn't endure watching the very sexy Carlotta, knowing
at Iain knew her well enough to call her "friend."

Carlotta. *Pow!* That earned another punch to the bag.
ani cocked her elbow again, then stumbled as a strong
nd wrapped around her arm and held her back.

"Enough, Kani," Bryan said quietly.

She smiled grimly. "I'll bet you've gotten really tired of
e moping around."

"I'm always concerned about you, especially the way you
o all or nothing into situations. Maybe you should call
fom and ask her to fly up tomorrow instead of waiting
ntil the weekend. I've got to leave town—"

"So leave. You've been gone off and on these last few
reeks. What's the difference?" She tugged off her boxing
loves and swept her sweatband off her head, running her
ngers through her hair.

"You've been so sure he was coming back. Now I think
ou've given up."

She shrugged. "I had hope until yesterday."

"What happened?"

"Corinne called again."

"How is she? What'd she say?"

"That they're getting along fine. She said something
bout Iain being grateful to you . . . ?"

"I found something he was looking for. No big deal," he
aid. "What else did she say?"

"He's asked her to live with him and go to school there,
nd she's agreed. So has Helena apparently. Not that
hey've given her much choice. He took her to meet their

father, but Darnell rejected her, a move that turned Iain int
her champion.''

"They can do DNA tests to be sure, you know. If she cal
again, you might suggest it.''

"She won't call.''

"Why not?''

Kani swept her towel off the floor and mopped her fac
and arms with it. "I asked her what he had to say about me
She said they never discuss me. If he won't even say m
name, what chance do you think I have of him seeing th
light? I really thought it would work out this time, Bryan
But obviously he didn't love me enough. As I've alway
said, I'm missing that something special it takes to hold o
to a man.''

"That's not true, sis. So you've given up?''

"For my own self-preservation, I have to. There's a ma
who's been coming to the city on business for the past thre
years, the first week of every month. He stays at the hote
comes to the bar late in the afternoon for a drink and con
versation. He's been wanting to take me out. I think thi
time I'll accept.''

"Why?''

"Why?'' She smiled wryly, then tapped a finger on hi
chest. "That's a very good question, brother dear. When
find the answer, I'll let you know.''

"Keep your head, Kani.''

"Why? I kept my head this time. Didn't put pressure o
him, didn't let myself believe it would work out between u
until I knew for sure I'd earned his trust and his love.
thought that this time I was doing everything right. I knov
he's not perfect. *But he's perfect for me.* Do you know, he'
the first man to accept me just the way I am. He's neve
tried to change me in any way. When I was being silly, h
didn't give me one of those looks that says 'Grow up.' Whe
I was sad, he just held me. When I was angry, he didn't tr
to tease me out of it. He *liked* my independence. He like
that I didn't defer to him all the time. And I liked that h
didn't expect me to.'' Tears overflowed her eyes. "Well, I'n

ne hoping. Now I'll grieve for a little while, then I'll go
. I've accepted an offer for Ramshackle that I can't pass
. It won't give me any money up-front, but the monthly
yments will be enough for me to buy a car and to do some
aveling, maybe take some classes at the university. I can-
t, will not, sit at home pining away."

"Excuse me, miss?"

Kani approached the woman just seating herself at the
r.

"May I have a glass of Chablis, please?"

The woman looked so out of place there that Kani alost refused to serve her, almost asked her to go into the
ning room, where Kani would have had the woman's wine
nt over. She was at least seventy years old and weighed no
ore than a hundred pounds. Her white hair was cropped
ort, permed tightly, and probably didn't lose its shape in
e wind. She was everyone's grandmother.

Kani poured the glass, then placed it and a napkin on the
unter.

"Thank you, miss."

"You're welcome."

"Um, could I ask a favor of you?"

"Me?" Kani asked in surprise.

The woman looked around, obviously counting the
umber of patrons in the lounge, which was not a stagger-
g amount. "Would it be possible, I mean, you see, I left
ome this morning without setting my VCR, and I never
iss my story, you know." She looked hopefully at Kani.

"You'd like me to turn the television on?"

"Yes, if you would, please. If you think the other cus-
mers won't mind."

Kani grinned. "Who cares? You asked, they didn't. What
hannel?"

"Channel 3. 'A Time to Love.'"

Kani stiffened. *You're being tested, Kani*, she told her-
elf. *Don't worry about it. Just walk over there and turn it*

*on. You won't die. You won't even pass out. Go on. Mov
your feet.*

"I'll get it, chickadee," Jake said, noting her hesitance

"I can do it," she said.

Fifteen minutes of the program had gone by. The scen
was one between Carlotta and a character Kani hadn't see
before....

"Doctor, I had a bizarre dream about people I don't eve
know. What does it mean when you dream about peop.
you've never met?" Carlotta said.

"Are you sure they were strangers to you?"

"Positive. The woman looked a little like m
but...sweeter, and her name was Kani. The man was a beac
bum named Iain."

Kani spun toward the television. She'd been determine
to ignore the show, had walked to the farthest point of th
bar but now was drawn back, mesmerized.

"Beach bum?" the doctor queried.

Carlotta waved a dismissive hand. "Sun-streaked hai
tall, tanned, athletic. You know."

"Ah, yes. I see. And so...?"

"So this man, Iain, was in a huge room, like a ballroom
He sat in the very center of the room, alone."

"Alienation and isolation," the doctor interpreted. ",
small person in a big space."

"He wasn't crying on the outside, but you could see he'
been crying on the inside. He'd lost something. Somethin
very precious to him, something he hadn't felt worthy o
having in the first place, but something he'd come to be
lieve he was entitled to."

"Self-rejection, self-acceptance. Important facets of th
human psyche."

"The man leaned his forehead against his knees for a lon
time. Then, when he lifted his head, he caught sight of th
woman, Kani. She was wearing a neon green bathing suit
Did I tell you he was wearing only a bathing suit, too? Sh
seemed to take forever to reach him. She walked ever s
slowly, as if she had all the time in the world. He wanted he

hurry, to run, but he couldn't say the words to her. He st mentally compelled her to come, not to stop, not to sappear.

"Finally she stood before him. 'I thought I'd lost you rever,' he said. 'You almost did,' she replied. 'You alost waited too long.' 'Almost?' he asked. She smiled at n. 'Almost.'"

"Wish fulfillment," the doctor said authoritatively.

"Suddenly, a chandelier appeared above them and the ost beautiful music drifted in. She held out her hand to n, and he took it and stood, then swept her into a waltz. eir bathing suits disappeared. His turned into an elegant xedo. Hers became the most beautiful wedding gown, with train twenty feet long that swirled around them as they oved. The sky above them turned black and the chander shattered into pieces, becoming stars of unmatched illiance. A moon with a smiling face shone down upon em and they both began to smile as their friends and mily appeared at the edge of the ballroom and moved toard them, applauding and cheering and whistling."

"Support of their peers. It's critical."

"Two little boys and two little girls dressed in white and oking like miniatures of Iain and Kani held hands in a rcle around them. The couple stopped dancing and ouched down to the children, drawing them within their ms and kissing them, making them laugh. And I think...I ink they lived happily ever after."

"So you believe in fairy tales."

"I haven't believed for a long time, Doctor. But this one emed so *real*."

"Real? Too many ifs were manifested in your dream. *If* is Iain believed that without this woman, Kani, he would alone for the rest of his life. If he honestly recognized he ad lost something of value. If he believed he was *truly* orthy of her, not merely telling himself so. If she would rgive him. If she hadn't given up on him. If she still loved m as he once believed. If she wanted to marry him as uch as he wanted to marry her. If she wanted to make ba-

bies and help them grow. If she wanted a family and a lif
time with him.''

"I know all of *his* ifs are truths. The only question
hers.''

The screen went fuzzy. Kani choked on a sob, her han
pressed to her mouth.

"Turn around, chickadee. Look over yonder.''

Kani spun around. Way down at the very end of t
lounge, Iain stood, leaning against the wall, his han
shoved into his pockets. It was a casual pose, but it did
fool her. He looked taut enough to break in two.

To get to the lift-top of the bar meant her exiting
quired spending extra time. Instead, she backed up a fe
steps, sprinted, planted her hands and vaulted over it in o
smooth movement. She watched him straighten, watch
him begin to move toward her as she ran toward him. F
opened his arms in time to catch her as she threw herself in
his embrace, and he spun her around and around, then s
her down gently to kiss her with tenderness and passion a
love.

"I love you, Kani. I love you.''

"I love you, too, Iain. I'll never stop.''

"Can you forgive me?''

"I'd forgive you just about anything, Iain. I love you.'

"I thought I'd die when I saw you fly over the bar,'' I
said, tucking her under his chin to savor her nearness. F
could hear the smile in her voice.

"I've always wanted to do that.'' She leaned back a li
tle. "Ask me yourself.''

"I love you, Kani Warner. Please, will you marry me?'

"I will.'' She grinned. "I want a big wedding, with all tl
trimmings.''

"Whatever you want. Just guarantee me, *guarantee* m
you'll never leave me.''

She cupped a hand to his cheek. "Is a lifetime guarant
long enough for you?''

"No. Beyond life, Kani.''

"An eternal guarantee?''

He nodded. "That's close."

"How'd you do that, with the show?"

"Videotape. You weren't watching the real show. I would have been here last week except for setting that up. I had to coordinate with so many people to pull it off. That was Wes's great-aunt Ethel who asked you to turn on the television. She thought it was so romantic."

She slugged his shoulder. "You made me wait—worry—all this time when you knew—knew!—you were coming back?"

His mouth quirked at her flash of fire. "I did."

"You creep!"

He held her head between his hands. "I wanted it to be memorable, something you could keep in your mental scrapbook forever. There were things I needed to say that I probably couldn't have articulated in front of you. What's a week out of a lifetime?"

She softened considerably. "You went to a lot of trouble for me, Hollywood."

"Yeah, well, you *are* a lot of trouble, but you're *my* trouble, and you're worth it." He hesitated; a frown settled on his face. "I don't know what kind of father I'll make. I didn't have much of a role model."

Kani pulled him down for a breathtaking kiss. "I have it on the highest authority that you'll be an outstanding father."

"Who says?"

"My mother."

"Your mother? But I haven't even met her."

"Ah, but a Gypsy told her."

"She goes to fortune-tellers?"

Kani laughed. "That wouldn't surprise me, but no, just one little Gypsy told her. I'll explain later. Where's Corinne?"

"Over standing with Bryan. See?" He spun her around. Bryan and Corinne were walking toward them.

"Were you part of this plot?" Kani asked her brother after hugging Corinne.

"Only since about two hours ago. He needed a VCR hooked up without your knowing it."

Iain smiled wryly. "He didn't give me any encouragement whatsoever. I didn't know how you felt about me after my weeks of silence, and he wasn't about to help me. I don't know what to say, Bryan, except thanks. No one's ever gone out of their way for me before."

"We're family now, Iain."

"Even me?" Corinne asked impertinently.

"Even you, little girl."

"Good," she said with a nod. "I like having a family."

Iain bent close to his love. "You can count on me, Kani."

"I never doubted it, Iain. I never doubted it."

* * * * *

COMING NEXT MONTH

Jilted!
They were left at the altar...
but not for long!

#889 THE ACCIDENTAL BRIDEGROOM—Ann Major

November's *Man of the Month* Rafe Steele never thought one night with Cathy Calderon would make him a father. Now he had to find her before she married someone else!

#890 TWO HEARTS, SLIGHTLY USED—Dixie Browning

Outer Banks

Frances Jones discovered the way to win sexy Brace Ridgeway was through his stomach—until he got the flu and couldn't eat! But by then, Brace only craved a sweet dessert called Frances....

#891 THE BRIDE SAYS NO—Cait London

Clementine Barlow gave rancher Evan Tanner a "Dear John" letter from her sister, breaking their engagement. Even though the bride said no, will this sister say yes?

#892 SORRY, THE BRIDE HAS ESCAPED—Raye Morgan

Ashley Carrington couldn't marry without love, so she ran off on her wedding day. Was Kam Caine willing to risk falling in love to give this former bride a chance?

#893 A GROOM FOR RED RIDING HOOD—Jennifer Greene

After being left at the altar, Mary Ellen Barnett knew she couldn't trust anyone. Especially the wolf that lay underneath Steve Rawlings's sexy exterior....

#894 BRIDAL BLUES—Cathie Linz

When Nick Grant came back home, Melissa Carlson enlisted his help to win back her ex-fiancé. But once she succeeded, she realized it was Nick she wanted to cure her bridal blues!

FREE TV 3268 DRAW RULES
NO PURCHASE OR OBLIGATION NECESSARY

50 Panasonic 13" Color TVs (value: $289.95 each) will be awarded in random drawings to be conducted no later than 1/15/95 from among all eligible responses to this prize offer received as of 12/15/94. If taking advantage of the Free Books and Gift Offer, complete the Official Entry Card according to directions, and mail. If not taking advantage of the offer, write "Free TV 3268 Draw" on a 3" X 5" card, along with your name and address, and mail that card to: Free TV 3268 Draw, 3010 Walden Ave., P.O. Box 9010, Buffalo, NY 14240-9010 (limit: one entry per envelope; all entries must be sent via first-class mail). Limit: one TV per household. Odds of winning are determined by the number of eligible responses received. Offer is open only to residents of the U.S. (except Puerto Rico) and is void wherever prohibited by law; all applicable laws and regulations apply. Names of winners available after 2/15/95 by sending a self-addressed, stamped envelope to: Free TV 3268 Draw Winners, P.O. Box 4200, Blair, NE 68009.

SWP-STV94

**The stars are out in October at Silhouette! Read
captivating love stories by talented *new* authors—
in their very first Silhouette appearance.**

Sizzle with Susan Crosby's
THE MATING GAME—Desire #888
...when Iain Mackenzie and Kani Warner are forced
to spend their days—and *nights*—together in *very* close
tropical quarters!

Explore the passion in Sandra Moore's
HIGH COUNTRY COWBOY—Special Edition #918
...where Jake Valiteros tries to control the demons that
haunt him—along with a stubborn woman as wild as the
Wyoming wind.

Cherish the emotion in Kia Cochrane's
MARRIED BY A THREAD—Intimate Moments #600
...as Dusty McKay tries to recapture the love he once
shared with his wife, Tori.

Exhilarate in the power of Christie Clark's
TWO HEARTS TOO LATE—Romance #1041
...as Kirby Anne Gordon and Carl Tannon fight for custody
of a small child...and battle their growing attraction!

Shiver with Val Daniels'
BETWEEN DUSK AND DAWN—Shadows #42
...when a mysterious stranger claims to want to save
Jonna Sanders from a serial killer.

Catch the classics of tomorrow—*premiering* today—
Only from

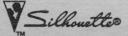

PREM94

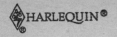 HARLEQUIN®   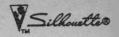 Silhouette®

The movie event of the season can be the reading event of the year!

Lights... The lights go on in October when CBS presents Harlequin/Silhouette Sunday Matinee Movies. These four movies are based on bestselling Harlequin and Silhouette novels.

Camera... As the cameras roll, be the first to read the original novels the movies are based on!

Action... Through this offer, you can have these books sent directly to you! Just fill in the order form below and you could be reading the books...before the movie!

48288-4	Treacherous Beauties by Cheryl Emerson	$3.99 U.S./$4.50 CAN.	☐
83305-9	Fantasy Man by Sharon Green	$3.99 U.S./$4.50 CAN.	☐
48289-2	A Change of Place by Tracy Sinclair	$3.99 U.S./$4.50CAN.	☐
83306-7	Another Woman by Margot Dalton	$3.99 U.S./$4.50 CAN.	☐

TOTAL AMOUNT	$
POSTAGE & HANDLING	$
($1.00 for one book, 50¢ for each additional)	
APPLICABLE TAXES*	$ _____
<u>**TOTAL PAYABLE**</u>	$ _____
(check or money order—please do not send cash)	

To order, complete this form and send it, along with a check or money order for the total above, payable to Harlequin Books, to: **In the U.S.:** 3010 Walden Avenue, P.O. Box 9047, Buffalo, NY 14269-9047; **In Canada:** P.O. Box 613, Fort Erie, Ontario, L2A 5X3.

Name: _____

Address: _____ City: _____

State/Prov.: _____ Zip/Postal Code: _____

*New York residents remit applicable sales taxes.
 Canadian residents remit applicable GST and provincial taxes.   CBSPR

"HOORAY FOR HOLLYWOOD" SWEEPSTAKES

HERE'S HOW THE SWEEPSTAKES WORKS

OFFICIAL RULES — NO PURCHASE NECESSARY

To enter, complete an Official Entry Form or hand print on a 3" x 5" card the words "HOORAY FOR HOLLYWOOD", your name and address and mail your entry in the pre-addressed envelope (if provided) or to: "Hooray for Hollywood" Sweepstakes, P.O. Box 9076, Buffalo, NY 14269-9076 or "Hooray for Hollywood" Sweepstakes, P.O. Box 637, Fort Erie, Ontario L2A 5X3. Entries must be sent via First Class Mail and be received no later than 12/31/94. No liability is assumed for lost, late or misdirected mail.

Winners will be selected in random drawings to be conducted no later than January 31, 1995 from all eligible entries received.

Grand Prize: A 7-day/6-night trip for 2 to Los Angeles, CA including round trip air transportation from commercial airport nearest winner's residence, accommodations at the Regent Beverly Wilshire Hotel, free rental car, and $1,000 spending money. Approximate prize value which will vary dependent upon winner's residence: $5,400.00 U.S.); 500 Second Prizes: A pair of "Hollywood Star" sunglasses (prize value: $9.95 U.S. each). Winner selection is under the supervision of D.L. Blair, Inc., an independent judging organization, whose decisions are final. Grand Prize travelers must sign and return a release of liability prior to traveling. Trip must be taken by 2/1/96 and is subject to airline schedules and accommodations availability.

Sweepstakes offer is open to residents of the U.S. (except Puerto Rico) and Canada who are 18 years of age or older, except employees and immediate family members of Harlequin Enterprises, Ltd., its affiliates, subsidiaries, and all agencies, entities or persons connected with the use, marketing or conduct of this sweepstakes. All federal, state, provincial, municipal and local laws apply. Offer void wherever prohibited by law. Taxes and/or duties are the sole responsibility of the winners. Any litigation within the province of Quebec respecting the conduct and awarding of prizes may be submitted to the Regie des loteries et courses du Quebec. All prizes will be awarded; winners will be notified by mail. No substitution of prizes are permitted. Odds of winning are dependent upon the number of eligible entries received.

Potential grand prize winner must sign and return an Affidavit of Eligibility within 30 days of notification. In the event of non-compliance within this time period, prize may be awarded to an alternate winner. Prize notification returned as undeliverable may result in the awarding of prize to an alternate winner. By acceptance of their prize, winners consent to use of their names, photographs, or likenesses for purpose of advertising, trade and promotion on behalf of Harlequin Enterprises, Ltd., without further compensation unless prohibited by law. A Canadian winner must correctly answer an arithmetical skill-testing question in order to be awarded the prize.

For a list of winners (available after 2/28/95), send a separate stamped, self-addressed envelope to: Hooray for Hollywood Sweepstakes 3252 Winners, P.O. Box 4200, Blair, NE 68009.

CBSRLS